WHO KNEW TASMANIAN TIGERS EAT APPLES?

BACK TO THE BEGINNING

WINDY MOUNTAIN
BOOK 6

JOHN MARTIN

ABOUT THE AUTHOR

John Martin is an Australian. He used to be a journalist, now he's free to be frivolous.

https://johnmartin-author.blog

CONTENTS

ONE
PERVERT OF INTEREST
LATE LAST CENTURY

SERGEANT RANDOLPH BIRTWISTLE wished now he hadn't left the shelter of the bar at that precise time.

If he hadn't been trying to beat the rain, he wouldn't now be standing in front of the bench, knowing full well who was sitting on the other side of that newspaper — but still feeling duty-bound to ask the question:

"Mr Mayor, is that you?"

Mayor James Northan lowered his rain-speckled newspaper. "So you *are* here, sergeant?"

Birty sighed. A few minutes earlier he had been warm and dry in the footy club bar after a heart-stopping victory by his old team, the Windy Mountain Tigers. But he had abandoned his glass of sarsaparilla when he glanced out the window and saw dark clouds gathering.

The ensuing 100-yard dash to the police station had been a cinch when he was younger and slimmer. But now it made him puff. The raindrops blurring his spectacles didn't make it any easier this afternoon.

It was a wonder he even noticed some idiot sitting on the bench on the grassy verge in the middle of the High Street. But his reflexes got the better of him, and he slid to a halt. By the time he took in the blue pin-stripe trousers, the shiny shoes and a masthead that told him the newspaper was *The Financial Review*, it was all too late.

"I've been trying to ring you all afternoon, sergeant." Even when Mayor Northan was looking up at him, he somehow made Birty feel he was looking down at him. "Has any progress been made on the missing telephone box?"

The mayor didn't wait for a reply. "If you were more in touch with the community, you'd know people use that phone box — old people especially."

When Birty sat down, the dampness seeped through the back of his pants. He closed his eyes and counted in his head … one, two, three … his missus had ironed these trousers! He sighed again. "You didn't get to the game?"

"I had better things to do." Mayor Northan stabbed a finger at the newspaper. "I found an interesting article on windsocks."

"More interesting than watching Windy Mountain win a place in the grand final? Moose Routley kicked the winning goal on the siren."

The mayor curled his lip. "Oh, for heaven's sake! That means I'll have to talk to the players in front of half the town!"

"If it's any consolation, I don't think you'll have to talk to Moose. Silly bugger got himself reported for punching an opponent."

Birty stood and reached behind to pinch back his trousers. "Sorry, but I have to get going. This rain is getting heavier." He could see beads of water on the mayor's nose now. "I really have to get to work for my very last night shift. The sooner I start—"

"I thought you had months to go?" Mayor Northan's eyes widened.

"No, only six more shifts. We're booked on a cruise in ten days' time." Birty removed his spectacles and wiped them with a hanky. "Rita's been asking me to take her on a South Pacific holiday for years."

"Don't you think sixty is a bit young to be retiring? You're only three years older than me." He gave a measured little smile — the kind he used when turning a gear in the background. "You're not thinking about another career, by any chance?"

Birty laughed as he put the glasses back on. "I'm planning on catching lots of trout."

"Pity. I could do with someone like you to help me with my new project." The mayor lowered his voice. "What would you say if I told you I've decided not to sell my orchard after all?"

"I'd say that would make a lot of people around here very happy."

"Would it?" The mayor smirked. "What I've decided to do now is hang on to the land, rip out the orchard and build a windsock factory on the site."

"How's that going to make things better?" Birty resumed his silent counting … five, six, seven … "That orchard is part of the heritage of this town. People won't let you tear it down."

"I've obviously misjudged you, sergeant. You're allowing senti-mentality to muddle your mind."

"Look, I've really gotta go, Mr Mayor. You'd better get some cover, too, before you catch your death." With that wishful thought, Birty crossed the road.

———

Birty heard Constable Smith and Junior Constable Stretch arrive about 6pm. Their boots squelched on the linoleum floor as they came down the hall.

Birty growled when he saw the trail of muddy footprints behind them when they came into the charge room. "I hope you young blokes haven't been drinking?"

"Of course not, sarge," Smithy said. "We only had a few lemonades to celebrate."

Birty tried to ratchet up his grumpy look so Smithy wouldn't be able to detect he shared his excitement. "Just as well I've decided to work one last Saturday, eh?"

"Thanks, sarge. I owe you."

"Just win the premiership. Then you can retire from the game on a high note."

Birty's mentors had schooled him in the art of tough love, which is how come he tried hard not to give the impression he thought much of the football skills of young Smithy.

He had to admit Smithy was a darn good ruckman. But he'd reached the same fork in the road Birty had come to 35 years earlier.

They had already had THE talk.

"You have to make up your mind." Birty tapped his index finger on Smithy's chest. "Do you want to hang with the boys every Saturday afternoon or do you want to further your career with the Police Force? Because. You. Can't. Do. Both."

Birty couldn't believe it was 1993 already. He had had his retirement date circled in his diary for years and now it was just about here. He had come to Windy Mountain nearly 40 years before as a junior constable. He had married a local girl and done his best to get involved in the community.

Most of the year Windy Mountain was a law-abiding little town, and Birty and Smithy didn't have to raise much of a sweat.

Except for the missing telephone box, and the frequent, but peaceful, locking up of The Big O, a copper's life around here was pretty quiet.

Smithy now had a new colleague. The idea was Smithy would step up to become station boss and Stretch would become his assistant. Stretch had never played football but Windy Mountain had already signed him for the next year on the thinking if he brought nothing else to the team at least he was big enough to get in his opponents' way. Birty wondered how long it would be before Smithy was thumping his finger on Stretch's chest during THE talk.

Then again, perhaps that would become a thing of the past. Policing had changed and he guessed it would continue to evolve. Birty remembered when it was quite acceptable for him to clip schoolboys under the ear if they were spotted smoking behind the changeroom sheds at the Football Ground or caught nicking fruit from

Northan's orchard. And everyone turned a blind eye if bully and petty thief Freddy Cuthbert was brought from the cells with a black eye.

All this political correctness and sticking to the rule book had been coming for years. Smithy would probably cope. But he was still going to have to hang up his boots at age 24.

Birty actually welcomed the arrival of the muddy boots. Mopping the floor would be a welcome break from trying to tidy up all his paperwork. That's another thing that bugged him these days. Were all these forms really necessary?

"You didn't see the Mayor across the road when you came in?" Birty said.

Smithy scoffed. "Are you joking? It's raining cats and dogs out there now!"

"You know the Mayor? He's so full of himself he probably thinks he can command the weather to change."

Smithy and Stretch wouldn't have heard him. They had turned around and were headed to the urn.

"Hey," Birty barked. "What do you think you're doing?"

"We're just making a drink, sarge."

"This isn't a blooming cafeteria! I want you two out on the street A.S.A.P. I don't want any over-zealous spectators thinking they can misbehave in this town."

Smithy looked at his watch. "You must have seen how many people were packed in the bar? If anyone's managed to cut through and order more than four beers by now, I'd be surprised. No one will be unruly at this hour, especially in this weather."

"Just do it, son, OK? When you've got your bum in this chair, you can do what you like. Right now . . . " He pointed to the mug beside him. It said in big letters: THE BOSS.

Smithy and Stretch put on their raincoats and went out. At 11pm they made their first arrest. But this one was expected on a Saturday night. They carried The Big O in and deposited him in the cell.

———

He was filling in the final minutes of his shift by trying to come up with a name for *The Pick Of The Crop's* cow when the front door slammed again.

Birty glanced up at the clock on the wall. It was nearly midnight.

The shouting and screaming and thump-thump-thumping noise was getting louder as it came up the corridor.

When Smithy came through the door to the charge room, he lowered his rain hood and smiled.

He was carrying a red apple and a yellow apple.

Trailing him was Stretch, who was handcuffed to a woman who was beating him with a handbag. She was as ugly as a hat full of arseholes.

Second thoughts, Birty realised it was actually a young man dressed in drag.

He was wearing thick makeup, a wig, a pink dress, green stockings and a pair of sand-shoes. Stretch was trying to shield his face with his free hand, but his shoulders and knuckles were taking a pounding.

The sergeant jumped to his feet. "Now stop that. I won't tolerate my constables being assaulted."

The man stopped in mid-wallop. "He called me a pervert."

"That's not correct, sarge," Smithy said. "We've gone by the book on this one, haven't we Stretch? We arrested this fellow riding a bicycle on the High Street."

He pulled a notebook out of his coat pocket and read from it in a monotone. "When the prisoner asked why he was being arrested, Junior Constable Stretch said he was *a person of interest*." He added, "Not a *pervert* of interest, sarge."

Birty scratched his head. Riding a bicycle while looking ugly wasn't actually a crime.

"Can we have a moment, Constable Smith?" Birty ushered Smithy to a corner where they turned their backs on the prisoner and Stretch.

"What was he doing wrong?" Birty whispered.

"He was dressed in women's clothing in public between the hours of sunset and sunrise. That's against the law in Tasmania."

Birty tugged at his dwindling strands of hair. He had booked drunks, traffic offenders, even a thief or two, but he had never had to deal with this type of thing.

He walked back over to the prisoner and eyed him up and down. He was about 5 foot 7.

"Take off that wig and let's get a proper look at you."

Birty felt a shower of water on his face as the wig came off. But before he could protest, he heard two thumps behind him. When he turned, Smithy looked stunned — as if he suddenly realised he knew this fellow. But he didn't say anything. He just stooped down to pick up the apples from the wooden floor.

"Sorry, sarge," he said when he stood back up. "Exhibit A and Exhibit B. He was wearing these inside his brassiere."

"For crying out loud." Now the prisoner was wig-less, Birty could see his short hair fell somewhere between blond and red-head. "You can't arrest me for stuffing apples down my front!"

"Don't start telling me what I can or can't do in my own police station," Birty said. "Don't you know it's against the law for men to wear women's clothes in public?"

"Between the hours of sunset and sunrise," Constable Smith added.

"I don't normally dress like this. I was riding my bike home from a football club fancy-dress party, trying to beat the rain squalls. It wasn't my fault my golden delicious fell out of my left cup. When I stopped to pick it up, these two blokes arrested me."

Birty eyed the prisoner up and down. "You're not from around here, are you son?"

"I come from Queensland. I live in Blackstump Road now."

Birty scratched his head. Blackstump Road was a few miles southeast of the town centre. The two run-down farmhouses along the road were now occupied by squatters.

Birty glanced at the clock again and it reminded him Rita had phoned 15 minutes before to say she was going to bed and was leaving his supper in the oven. It was drying up with every second.

So much for hoping for a nice quiet start to his final week in the job!

He went to the counter, opened the charge book, then picked up a pen. "OK, son, what's your name?"

"Les . . . Les Johnson. But everyone calls me Johnno. Why are you writing that down?"

"*I'm* asking the questions. Age?"

"Twenty-four."

Occupation?"

"I'm an assistant Tasmanian Tiger hunter." The prisoner craned his neck to see what the sergeant was writing.

Birty looked around and growled. "A what?"

"I'm helping Moose Routley to find Tasmanian Tigers."

"Moose Routley the footballer?"

"Same bloke."

"What's he doing searching for a dead animal?"

"He says there is a good chance it still lives."

"Does he just? I'd say he'd get better odds on beating that striking charge from today."

———

The sergeant walked ahead along the corridor. He unlocked the outer cell door, then stepped aside to let Smithy and Stretch go past with their prisoner.

He then squeezed by them and opened a steel door. "Hopefully a night in here will help you come to the conclusion your type is not welcome in this town. In you go . . . mind your head."

He pointed to somewhere in the gloom. "You'll find a clean blanket on that bed."

When they returned to the charge room, Smithy and Stretch walked over to the urn, but Birty called them back.

"You looked like you knew him, Smithy?"

"Only when he took off his wig, sarge. I've seen him around the footy club with Moose."

Birty scratched his head. "Did you know Moose was a Tasmanian Tiger hunter?"

He shook his head. "We assumed he was a hippy. Tiger even had to find him some boots so he could play."

———

Johnno pounded on the door and hollered through the peephole.

"Let me out . . . there's been a misunderstanding."

The next second, he jumped when someone pinched his bottom, and he nearly banged his head on the low sloping ceiling.

"What the . . . ?" He swung around with a swish of his dress. He couldn't see anyone. The room had a cold chill. The only illumination came from a low-watt lightbulb recessed into the ceiling, and he squinted into the semi-darkness. He could hear heavy breathing, and as his eyes adjusted he could make out a dark shape on one of the two beds, the one on the left. The shape's chest was rising up and down in time to light snoring. Or *pretend* snoring?

Johnno walked over and prodded the man in the ribs. "How do you like it? Not so funny now, is it?"

The man opened his eyes, gasped and sat bolt upright, blasting Johnno with alcohol fumes.

"Jesus, Mary, and Joseph." The man made the sign of the cross then covered his eyes. "A lady! Here!"

Johnno held up the wig. "Can't anyone tell the difference between a bloke and a sheila in this town?"

The man examined Johnno more closely as if he were trying to make out something in the fog.

"Oh, tank the Lord, you're a fella."

The man spoke with an Irish accent. He had at least one double chin — perhaps more, it was hard to tell in this dark room. He was bald but he had stubble on his face. He wore a khaki jumper and a pair of paint-speckled green and brown corduroy trousers with a rope for a belt. He swung his feet around and to the floor and eyed his new cell-mate up and down. "But . . . but . . . why are you wearing a dress?"

"It's a free world. I can wear what I like, can't I?"

"Well . . . no, not here . . . I tink Tasmania has a law prohibiting men from wearing dresses . . . Why did you wake me?"

"I roused you, mate, because somebody pinched me."

"Pinched you? Pinched you where?"

"You must already know that because you're the only one in here."

"I was sound asleep, I was, until you prodded me." He put out his hand. "I'm Father Ryan O'Shannessy."

"You're a priest?"

"Well, an EX-priest. Now I'm the town drunk. Everyone calls me The Big O."

Johnno shook the hand tentatively. "Say, you're not the bloke who saw a Tasmanian Tiger in the main street?"

"Noooo. Dat was one of my predecessors." He pointed to a long list of names gouged into the green paint that covered the brick walls. Johnno could just make it out at the top. *Wish-Wash, first guest of this cell, July 1965.*

"Someone told me this cell was used to house Irish convicts in the 1840s."

The drunk/priest laughed. "Far as I know I'm the only Irishman who's stayed here." He pointed again. "Dat's my name right under Brian Jacobs. He was a regular guest here, God rest his soul. Birty locked Brian up so often, it's a wonder he hasn't come back to haunt the place. Have you not run into Wish-Wash around the town? Big fella who wears loud clothes, laughs like a donkey?"

"No, but I'm only fairly new to the area. Why would someone pull my leg about the age of these cells?"

The Big O shook his head. "You sure you haven't met Wish-Wash? You can still see the ruins of the old convict cells near Northan's orchard. But I wouldn't go poking around dare in the dark — not unless you're happy to run into the ghost of Colonel Northan."

Johnno sat down on the side of his bed. He inspected the putrid blue cover and saw it encased a thin rubber mattress, which he lifted to reveal the concrete slab underneath.

"If it wasn't you who pinched me, who did?"

"You can see dare's nowhere for anyone to hide."

"Are you saying I imagined it?"

"All I'm saying is it wasn't me. Why would I do dat? I was sound asleep. The last ting I remember is being evicted from the bar at half-time of the footy and lying down somewhere."

Johnno folded his arms. The cell stank of urine, disinfectant and booze. His nose led his eyes to the stainless steel toilet in the corner. He looked up to a tiny window with bars high on the end wall, where the sloping ceiling was at its highest. He couldn't see the rain outside but he could hear it.

TWO
STILL LIFE WITH TELEPHONE BOX

THE BIG O woke up at dawn when light flooded in through the high window. Johnno hadn't slept a wink so he watched him emerge from deep slumber. Now Johnno could see his silvery stubble, he guessed the priest/drunk was in his late fifties or early sixties.

The men sat on their beds and talked.

"You don't have to call me Father O'Shannessy all the time. I'm used to being called The Big O."

"Why? Do you sing?"

"Goodness, no. But they're big on nicknames in this town. God knows what dey used to call me behind my back after mass!"

They whiled away some hours talking, but when they heard a jangle of keys and the lock being turned, Johnno looked up to see Sergeant Birtwistle in the doorway. He was wearing jeans and a checked flannel shirt.

He handed Johnno an envelope.

"What's this?" Johnno stared down at the envelope in his hands.

"It's a summons. You are required to appear at the Windy Mountain Magistrate's Court at 2 o'clock tomorrow afternoon." Birty rubbed his eyes.

The Big O got off his bed. "Aren't you going to give Johnno time to sign the wall?"

"He's had all night to do that." Birty looked from face to face. "Come on now, I'm in a hurry. It's really my day off."

Birty handed Father O'Shannessy his summons. He didn't even open it, and Johnno looked at him quizzically.

"What? Oh, dis?" The priest/drunk waved the unopened envelope. "When I lived in a house I couldn't afford to wallpaper my parlour. Now I've got all the bits of paper I need, I haven't even got a house any more."

———

Johnno tried to hold the dress up as he pedalled home. But he couldn't stop the hem from dipping into puddles as he rode the bumps.

Now no ratepayers lived in Blackstump Road, the council didn't bother mending any of the potholes. This lack of maintenance also explained why the sides of the road were overgrown with so many blackberry bushes.

Once he passed the Brian Jacobs Memorial Commune, the old Cameron farmhouse came into sight over the crest of the hill. Johnno freewheeled down into the gully.

The single-storey house badly needed work. The weatherboards were yellowing and the roof had faded to a rusty pink. The verandah needed shoring up.

You couldn't see all of the ramshackle sheds from here because most of them were behind the house. The Cameron family had moved on years before. Nobody knew who owned the property now. But it was home for Johnno, Moose, Lozza and Foetus.

Johnno dodged the fresh wheelbarrow ruts coming down the hill, and at the bottom of the gully crossed the rickety wooden bridge over the creek. When he dismounted at the gate, Acid and Anti-Acid welcomed him with barks as they strained on their chains.

As Johnno wheeled his bike around the side of the house, two chooks wandered across the yard, stopping every few steps to peck the ground for seed.

He dodged around the wheelbarrow laden with firewood and caught sight of the back of Moose.

The big man turned. His face was red and sweaty, and Johnno realised he was carrying an armful of firewood.

"Where have you been?"

"In jail. Thanks to you."

Moose threw the wood on the woodpile. "Me?"

"You didn't tell me it's illegal to wear drag in this town at night?"

"Oh, no. No way are you pinning that on me." He held up both palms. "I didn't make you dress up like that." He dropped his hands and put them on his hips. "Anyway, you picked a fine time to go AWOL" He started back towards the wheelbarrow.

"It was *your* after-match party, remember?" Johnno shouted to his back. Moose was always doing this to Johnno. "I dunno what you're going to do if the Tigers win the premiership next week-end. They're going to expect you to make an appearance for a change."

Moose was making a return trip with another bunch of firewood. His voice crackled as he passed. "Good thing I'll probably get rubbed out by the tribunal then."

"You don't know that? I'm sure the club is already planning your defence."

Moose threw to wood down and turned. "Why would they waste the energy? Everyone knows I hit him. The umpire was right there."

"What were you thinking?"

"He hand-balled over my head and I hate looking silly."

"But did you have to biff him?"

"What can I say? I had another rush of blood to the head."

"But did you have to punch him right in front of the umpire?"

Moose mopped his brow with his sleeve, and shrugged. "The team is good enough to win without me."

"You think?"

Moose glanced at his watch. "I had hoped to have gone bush by now."

Johnno's face dropped even more. "You're going hunting without me?"

"I need some time alone. My head is still pounding from the drama yesterday and then the drama we had here last night."

"Worse than being in jail?"

"Ask Foetus? I'd guess he's been locked up in jails lots of times. But I doubt he's been locked up in a hospital before."

Johnno's eyes opened wide. "Foetus is in hospital?"

"Lozza and I had a hell of a time getting him there."

"What's wrong with him?"

"By now? Who knows? Ask Lozza. She's had a miraculous recovery from her injury and is around the back painting."

————

Johnno found Lozza with her easel set up in front of the telephone box.

She looked up from her stool when she heard the soft whirr of the bike wheels. "You promised to take care of my dress!"

He handed her the summons. As she read it, her frown turned into a smirk.

"What's so funny?"

Lozza handed the summons back. Johnno could see she was biting her lip in an attempt not to laugh.

"Moose and I could have done with your help last night."

"So he said. He said you had to take Foetus to hospital?"

Lozza brushed her lip. "Moose is not even talking to me! Anyone would think I was always asking him to help me fetch the water from the creek?"

"Still got a sore wrist then?"

"I've got a certificate for two weeks' off work." She stood up. "I'll fill you in about Foetus inside."

They wiped their shoes on a mat on the back step and entered the house through a tatty fly-wire door. Inside, the kitchen fire in the wood stove radiated its heat. Lozza's frilly undies and other garments were drying on a clothes-horse. Johnno poured water from a red bucket into the kettle, then sat down on one of the wooden chairs around the table.

"When Moose and I got back from the footy yesterday, Foetus was lying on his bed moaning," Lozza said. "His skin was all yellow. I don't know how Moose persuaded Foetus to let us take him to the Windy Mountain Hospital, but he did and they admitted him on the spot. But you know Foetus? He tried to escape, slipped and hurt his ankle. The doctor thought it was broken but the X-rays show it's just badly sprained."

"How long will he be in?"

Lozza shook her head. "My bet is he'll wear out his welcome in no time."

Johnno yawned. "I'm knackered. Next time Moose pulls out of a fancy dress night, remind me to stay home too."

The water started to boil and Johnno got up.

"Not only do I have to go to court, somebody pinched my bottom in jail. Do you know how humiliating that is?"

He poured water into the teapot, waiting for a reaction. When it didn't come, he said, "Aren't you going to ask me who pinched my bottom?"

"Mr Nobody?"

Johnno's eyes widened. "How did you know that?"

"Now you know what it's like to wear a dress around here."

He sat back down, and thought it wise to change the subject. "Don't you think you've painted that telephone box enough?"

Lozza had already used her artistic talents to brighten up the exterior of the box, which now served a new life as a dunny. Moose had carved a toilet seat from Huon pine. Johnno had donated a bicycle bell which could be rung from inside to warn anyone heard approaching the telephone box was already engaged. Foetus hadn't done anything. But he was given the job of emptying the drum each week, so he had really drawn the short straw.

"I've decided to feature it in a series of paintings," Lozza said. "Like Van Gogh did with sunflowers . . . still life with telephone box."

She poured the tea with her good hand, and slid a mug over to Johnno.

He yawned again. "If you don't mind, I'll go and have some kip after I drink this. Wake me up in a couple of hours and I'll go visit Foetus."

———

He splashed his face with water from the bowl in the bathroom.

The bathroom was chockers with stuff, most of it beauty products belonging to Lozza. The blokes had shaving mugs. Moose shaved off his beard periodically and mailed the whiskers off so they could be fobbed off to American souvenir hunters. He had tried to persuade Foetus to do likewise. But the ex-bikie argued his beard was the last remnant of his motorcycle career and it would be like sending his left testicle to the United States and saying it came from a bushranger. He argued it would be much better to wait until Johnno could grow something better than bum-fluff on his face.

Johnno gave his teeth a quick brush. It was a shame the house didn't have running water. He spat into the washing bowl, then retreated to the bedroom he shared with Foetus.

Johnno kicked off his sand-shoes and wriggled out of Lozza's pink dress. He found a pair of shorts on the floor and slipped them on. He pulled on a reasonably clean T-shirt, laid back on his unmade bed, and dozed off.

THREE

SEND IN THE COW, THERE OUGHT TO BE COWS

IT WASN'T NORMAN J. Hit's idea to investigate the wind. He was given that assignment by the editor.

Ideas sprung from Dobber Leggs like bullets being shot up in the air. If he hit on anything, it was as accidental as something falling from the sky.

He was proud he led a newspaper tough on crime, strong on commerce, and which fully backed the man in charge of the town. When the Mayor had announced he was planning to sell his family orchard, Mr Leggs wrote an editorial applauding what he called a visionary plan that would set the town free from the ball and chain of sentimental nonsense. The newspaper also gave its unequivocal support to Mayor Northan's other project of passion. He was trying to get his council colleagues to use taxpayers' money to pay for an expensive larger-than-life bronze statue of his great, great, great grandfather that would stand in the middle of the High Street, opposite the council chambers, in place of the Colonel Richard Northan memorial park bench, which would be relocated to the outskirts of town. Suddenly, nostalgia was a good thing in the eyes of Dobber Leggs. He editorialised heritage was something Windonians should be proud of.

One day, he called Norman into his office.

It was the first time the rookie had been called into the editor's office, so this was a big deal.

Dobber Leggs looked at him over the top of his half-moon glasses.

"Norman, I've got a special assignment for you . . . I want you to find out where the wind comes from."

Norman couldn't believe his ears.

"The wind is one of the great discussion points of our society," the editor said. "Our readers talk about the wind in the pub, at the football, and in the hair salons. They want to know more about the wind, and I think you're just the young fellow to get to the bottom of it for them."

"But-but-but . . ."

"No buts, my boy. I want you to make a note of this."

Norman took out his notebook and his pen.

The editor peered thoughtfully at a blank spot high on the wall and ran his fingers over his chin. "I want to know where the wind comes from." Norman started to scribble down his words. "Does the world only have a certain amount of wind? If it's windy in Windy Mountain does that mean it's calm up at Slutz Plains? If Windy Mountain isn't windy where the heck does all that blustery air go? Get the idea?"

What happened the next day was just as surreal.

Dobber Leggs called everyone in the office together with the aim of brainstorming the best ways to boost circulation for the newspaper. Everyone from executives to the copyboy stood in a circle around the editor who stood near the chief-of-staff's desk. But nothing they suggested got any traction with him.

"I know!" he said when their ideas stopped coming and he looked at all those wish-this-would-end faces. "We'll give away a cow at the grand final."

Nobody in Windy Mountain raised cows. Apples, yes. Pears, yes. Sheep, only for the mountain oysters. But cows? Nobody kept cows!

Dobber Leggs's plan was this: For a reader to be in the running for a fine Friesian milking cow, all he or she had to do was correctly guess the name of the cow and say in 50 words or less why *The Pick Of The Crop* was their favourite family newspaper.

Dobber Leggs hoped to draw the winner on the half-forward flank of the football ground during halftime of the grand final. He told his chief-of-staff, Reg Collins, to make the arrangements.

———

"GIVE ME a jug of apple cider and a plate of fried mountain oysters." Oodles Noodles stood at the counter opposite publican Artie Rogerson.

Oodles, sixty-one, was the works foreman at the Windy Mountain Council.

A jukebox in the corner of the smoky room was playing *Laddi's Skammastu þín svo!* — the Icelandic version of Joe Dolce's Australian hit *Shaddup Your Face* — and Oodles slowly rolled a fag while he waited for his order. Buggered if he knew where he had put his pipe. He inspected the freshly rolled ciggie, and it really wasn't bad for someone so much out of practice. He popped the fag in his mouth, lit it, dragged deeply and exhaled with satisfaction.

He looked around. The bar of The Applecart was about 10 yards long with eight stools all occupied with relatively sober people. By mid arvo, Oodles knew they would all be drunk, and inflicted by football fever. Would Moose Routley get off? Could the team win without him? If he was rubbed out, how much would Slutz Plains win by?

Huddled around a table near the jukebox were the four greenies from the Brian Jacobs Memorial Commune. It was the second Sunday in a row Oodles had seen them in here.

Rog plonked the jug and mountain oysters down on the towelling mat. "Fresh out of the oven."

Oodles look down at them. "Christ, I asked for fried ones."

"But these ones are on the house."

"You mixed up the order, didn't you?"

"See, this is the thanks I get for being kind-hearted. If I had wanted to mix up the order don't you think I'd have given you the ones cooked in garlic so I could really annoy you?"

"You're not still trying to flog those!" Oodles screwed up his face. "Name me one person in town who even likes garlic?"

"I bet Tiger Kowalski would appreciate fine cuisine. With any luck, he'll bring his dago mates in some time." He looked down at the plate on the counter. "Trust you to look a gift mountain oyster in the mouth, Oodles. I just thought you'd like baked ones to impress that new bloke you have with you. The cider is on the house too."

"You've never shouted us before!"

"How remiss of me! You and Wish-Wash are such good customers. Wish-Wash especially!" He paused, then said, "I'm guessing the young fellow with you is the new cop."

"Oh, I get it now. Nothing to do with me or Wish-Wash. It's him you are trying to sweeten up, eh? Stop him from snooping?"

"You know how it is? A publican couldn't keep his head above water if he went strictly by the book. Best to stay on the right side of the constabulary."

"If you really must know, Stretch is my new boarder. And, yes, he is the new young junior constable."

Rog grinned and clapped his hands. "I knew it. Only a cop would have a haircut like that! Do me a favour, Oodles? Make sure you tell him these were on me."

Oodles glared at him.

Rog's smile disappeared. "Well, it worked with old Birty. He hasn't been around for years."

"That's because you gave him food poisoning." Oodles peered down disapprovingly again at the plate.

"It wasn't deliberate, mate. Besides, he wouldn't still be doing all that fishing if it had lasting effects."

"Good point. Can you whip up another batch of bad ones and I'll home deliver them? I can tell him it's your Police Benevolent Day contribution."

Everyone knew Oodles and Birty were engaged in an epic wager.

For years now they had been in pursuit of a wily rainbow trout they had dubbed George, which had been often spotted, once hooked but never landed. George would be as tough and tasty as a sand-shoe by now, but it was the principle of the thing. Oodles, who had come to fly-fishing late in life, didn't want that fat, old copper to get the better of him. Birty probably had cabinets full of trophies. He was always crowing about what a good footballer he had been. He had been fly-fishing a lot longer, too.

Oodles moved to Tasmania from Melbourne when he was thirty-eight.

First came the job, then the house and then his Sunday school habit.

Oodles was probably the oldest hoon in town but he always left his car in the garage on Sundays, and strolled into town with Madge. She kissed him goodbye outside The Applecart and continued on to the Catholic church for mass.

The Applecart didn't actually have a licence to open on the sabbath, but they got around it by calling the session Sunday School. As long as you were over 18, you were welcome to worship a few glasses of cider, play poker with the blokes and unwind ahead of another hard week of yakka.

Madge didn't mind as long as Oodles came home after lunch in a fit-enough state to help her in the garden.

Only twice in 25 years had he forgotten. It was an easy mistake to make when you've had a skin full. One minute you're having a quiet little drink and a game of cards with the boys, time gets away from you and next thing you look out the window and see it's dark already. Bugger it, you decide. It's a little-known fact the worst gardening injuries occur at night. Then Rog asks you if you want another drink and the next minute you are taking a phone call from Madge and everyone can hear her admonishing you on the phone, using your full name, which the regulars often now reminded him was Clarence John Noodle.

Rog didn't seem to appreciate the look Oodles was giving the plate of baked mountain oysters. "I can give them to someone else!"

"What? And miss winning a copper for a friend? I think it's going to take more than one plate though. You better keep them coming. Fried next time though. And more cider."

"Don't push your luck, Oodles. I'm not made of money."

Pull the other one, thought Oodles. Everyone knew Rog brewed his own cider illegally, thus avoiding tax and excise. God knows where the money went? He had to be raking in enough to offset giving away a few measly freebies.

"Up to you. But don't say I didn't warn you. Never know when you might need a friend in blue."

"You're forgetting Birty and me are like this?" Rog held up two crossed fingers.

"Fat lot of good that'll do you soon. The blind bandicoot retires at the end of the week." He shook his head. "The worse thing is he has got a good year on me before I retire and he'll probably be bush every night and day in his waders until he hooks George."

Oodles picked up the freebies in either hand and headed back to the table with his fag dangling from his mouth.

"Don't forget to tell the young cop these are on the house?" he heard Rog say behind him

Oodles weaved around five tables, including the eight-ball table, and dodged a wayward dart but plonked the jug and plate down on the table.

Wish-Wash frowned. "What was Rog on about? I saw him shouting after you but I couldn't hear what he said with all this noise."

"Beats me. I asked for fried mountain oysters and he got the order mixed up. My guess is he was saying the next lot would be on the house."

Stretch did have the look of a copper, despite being dressed this morning in a blue checked flannel shirt. Rog had been spot-on about the short back and sides haircut being a dead giveaway. But his lanky frame was a decent clue, too — he looked like a puppy who had yet to grow into his enormous feet. Stretch took a sip from his cider and picked up his story where he had left off when Oodles went up to the bar. "This bloke reckoned he was on his way home from a fancy dress party."

"He was probably just having a bit of innocent fun." Oodles blew a jet of smoke out from his nose.

"That's not what Sergeant Birtwistle thought," Stretch said. "This Johnson bloke really got on the sergeant's wick. He locked him up for the night."

"On what charge?" Wish-Wash put his cigarette down on the ashtray and picked up a mountain oyster.

"Dressing as a woman in public between sunset and sunrise," Stretch said.

Oodles nearly choked on the mountain oyster he was chewing.

"Madge dresses up as a woman in public every day and no one's had the good sense to lock *her* up," he said.

"If you ask me," whispered Wish-Wash in Stretch's direction, "you should be locking up those greenies. Just look at them…" He glanced to his left, ". . . drinking our cider and causing trouble."

"What trouble?" Stretch whispered back.

"It's a waste of a good crop of apples." The colour of Wish-Wash's face almost matched his trousers. Who knew the St Vinnies opportunity shop sold cheap fire-engine red trousers?

The greenies had never harmed Oodles. Besides, Wish-Wash, aged fifty-eight, had spent more than an hour at the greenies' table the previous Sunday. They had wanted to know about the night he saw the Tasmanian Tiger and it appeared to Oodles that Wish-Wash, as always, had been very happy to tell them all.

"What have the greenies ever done to you, Wish-Wash?" Stretch frowned.

"They're bludgers. You know how you can tell they're up to no good?" He nodded towards them. "It's when they leave on their beanies like that, like they're some kind of thinking caps."

"Oh, go easy on them, cobber." Oodles started shuffling the cards. "Did you get out of the wrong side of the bed this morning? I saw you looking daggers at The Big O."

Stretch squinted. "Who's The Big O?"

"Father O'Shannessy," Oodles said. "He's sitting over there on Wish-Wash's old stool."

Stretch gasped. "The priest is back here? He was blind drunk when we picked him up in the High Street last night. I would have thought a night in the cells might have taught him a lesson."

"It's his job to be here," Wish-Wash said.

"Steady," Oodles said. "You'll be defending the greenies next."

———

WISH-WASH was correct. The greenies were hatching a plan. They had been told the endangered Green Swift Parrot had begun nesting in the trees at the Northan apple orchard, and they were trying to decide what they needed to do about it. The fact a *For Sale* sign was hanging from the chain blocking the access road made them even more fearful. What if an ecologically unfriendly multi-national company bought the property?

"It's settled then," William Archibald-Smith said above the noise of the jukebox, which was now playing a French version of *Shaddup Your Face*, Sheila's *Et ne la ramène pas*.

"No, it is not." Dilly Brown's nostrils flared. "Why don't you go find yourself a nice safe office job, William? If you had any strength in your convictions, you wouldn't be scared about getting your hands dirty."

"I'm not scared," William said. "What don't you understand about the need for conservationists to work smarter and adopt more socially responsible tactics? I think the Green Swift Parrot is worth fighting for but I don't think we should break the law to do so."

Dilly looked up at the ceiling. "Who made you chairman anyway? Surely we've got more important things to worry about than this?"

"But," John Nitram said, "haven't we got an obligation to protect rare birds?"

"You suck hole," Dilly snapped.

"No need to be nasty," William said. "You do know John did his thesis on conservation? He has every right to voice a considered opinion."

"His opinion? Or parroting your opinion?" Dilly said. "Look, we're not talking about whitewater rivers or unique rainforests here. We're discussing the future of a bird which may or may not live in an apple orchard, for goodness sake."

She turned around and glared at the jukebox. "What *is* this music?"

William had claimed leadership of the Brian Jacobs Memorial Commune after the former head of the greenies was killed. The job came with the master bedroom and Brian's former partner, Sarah Sarandon. William was the longest-standing member of the commune but he had missed out on the charisma gene. He was short, bespectacled, his favourite colour was mission brown, his father was an accountant and his grandfather was an accountant.

He was always at loggerheads with the commune's newest member. Dilly had been a very active participant in radical politics at university, where she had majored in Women's Affairs. Apart from being a feminist, she was proud to call herself a Tasmanian Aborigine.

"Would we have to stand in front of bulldozers again, man, after what they did to Brian?" John asked.

"I'm not chaining myself to an apple tree planted by a male capitalist pig," Dilly said. "Not for a silly bird that is probably not even there."

"How many times do I have to tell you?" William took a deep breath. "My way, nobody has to chain themselves to any trees. And I think you're missing the point, Dilly. The Green Swift Parrot symbolises what we are fighting for: to protect our delicate ecosystem from man's excesses."

"But bulldozers aren't fair," complained Sarah, a dizzy blonde who had been Brian's girlfriend since they met at the Franklin blockade. "Brian's death was such a waste."

"I can't believe you're saying that?" Dilly said. "Did you enjoy him pinching your bottom in public all the time?"

"You're jealous," Sarah said.

"Is that what you think? Did I sound jealous when I told him to take his lecherous hand away from me before I cut his balls off?"

William tugged at a lock of his hair. "Trust you, Dilly, to throw in a grenade to confuse the issue. Whatever his human failings, Brian was a martyr for the cause."

"He was a serial pervert," Dilly said.

"They still dammed that creek," John said.

"Yes, well we need to tweak the way we do things," William said. "But, on the positive side, they now know they can't mess with us."

"You can't be serious?" Dilly glared at him. "When they finished with Brian he had track marks where his head used to be."

"That's an awful thing to say, Dilly." Sarah pulled a hanky from her handbag.

William waved his hands. "Good one, Dilly! I move we adjourn and revisit this discussion tonight after dinner."

FOUR
CLOSE SHAVE WITH BIG BOB

FOETUS KNEW POUTING WASN'T a good look for a bikie but he couldn't help it as he sank back into his pillow, and clenched his eyes shut.

This was all Moose's fault. Foetus hadn't even wanted to come to hospital. But Moose had got heavy with him.

He was examined by a young doctor, who ran tests in emergency, asked all kinds of questions, then declared he was going to admit Foetus.

"Pig's arse! All I need is a decent night's sleep. I can get that at home."

"I can't let you go . . ." — the doctor looked at the patient card — ". . . Mr, er, Foetus. You're delirious."

They made him ride in a wheelchair to the main part of the hospital where he was taken to an office to be processed by the head nurse.

Sister Daisy Rowbottom's hoity-toity voice reminded him of a school teacher he once wanted to rip the head off to make her shut the fuck up. The head nurse had eyed him up and down and said they'd have to find him something more appropriate to wear rather than dirty jeans and a leather jacket.

Foetus had waggled a finger at her. "I always need to be dressed to go at a moment's notice. My gang is coming back for me."

"My hospital, my rules, Mr Foetus."

That's when he had tried to bolt. He should have been more careful leaping out of the wheelchair. The next thing he was writhing in pain on the floor.

This had meant he wasn't going anywhere except to the X-ray room and then casualty where his ankle was bandaged.

Two hours later he was back where he started.

Sister Rowbottom wheeled him over to an open cupboard, where all the community pyjamas and gowns were kept. But he still refused to have a bar of any of them.

"Have it you own way, Mr Foetus." She walked back to her desk and dialled her phone. "Bob, can you drop what you're doing. I need you here."

Foetus had thought he and Moose were the biggest men in this town, but this orderly turned out to be way bigger. He also appeared to have more tattoos on his arms.

Big Bob had taken Foetus in an elevator up to a two-bed room on the second floor and no one had bothered him all night — except his whiny roommate.

"What are you looking at?" Foetus had said when Big Bob had left.

"N-n-nothing." Bubby Throsby, twenty-six years and nine stone wringing wet, didn't seem to be sick at all. He was being observed by medical staff for a few days. "The doctor says I can go home soon. He thinks I'm looking better."

"That so?" Foetus growled. "Want me to change that?"

Bubby didn't make a peep for the rest of the night. Whether he slept a wink was a moot point but at dawn he got up and left the room. He returned half an hour later full of new energy and talked and talked and talked.

After breakfast Big Bob had returned holding a box. Foetus watched in alarm as he closed the curtain around his bed and unpacked a cut-throat razor, a towel and some shaving cream.

"I think you have the wrong patient, mate."

Bob took a note out of his pocket and looked at it. "No. You're the bloke I wheeled up here yesterday? Foetus? It says here you need your groin to be prepped."

Foetus felt his heart skip a beat. "Is this Nurse Rowbottom's way of getting back at me?"

Bob smiled as he unsheathed the razor. "Don't worry, I'm pretty nimble for someone my size. But you'll need to be very still. If I slice into your femoral artery, we'll both know about it."

———

SOME hours later, Johnno arrived.

He dragged a chair nearer to the bed. "I thought they'd have you in a gown by now." Then he saw the sweat on Foetus's brow. "Crikey, you really aren't well!"

"They're trying to bring down my temperature with pills. Tell Lozza to bake some hash cookies. I need something stronger."

Johnno sat down and looked over to the other empty bed. "Where's your roommate?"

"I think he's gone for a bath," Foetus said. "With any luck someone will hold his head underwater."

Johnno exhaled. "How did you sleep?" Before Foetus could answer, he said, "Only I didn't sleep at all because I spent the night in jail."

"You!" Foetus lifted his head weakly and smirked. "What for?"

"Don't ask." Johnno made theatre by rolling his eyes. "The charge was so ridiculous, it wouldn't surprise me if they drop it in court."

"What's the big deal in not telling me then?"

"Someone might hear."

Foetus looked around. "Who's here to hear? If it makes you feel any better, come closer and whisper it to me."

That's what Johnno did, which made it more surprising when Foetus pushed him away mid-way through the story.

When he regained his balance, Johnno said, "Why did you do that?"

"I can't believe I've been sharing a room with a pervert!" Foetus's eyes were at full stretch.

"It was a *fancy-dress* party."

"But why couldn't you have gone as a bloke? What if someone had come into the room just now? They might have thought you were nibbling my ear!" Foetus put two fingers in his mouth.

"See, I knew you'd over-react. I could have lied and said I killed someone, and I'm sure you would have taken that better. Let's change the subject, shall we?"

Foetus coughed and coughed. Putting his fingers down his throat couldn't have helped. "Let me guess why Moose isn't with you. He's probably worried I'd have my strength back so he can't push me around any more?"

Johnno shook his head. "Actually he's gone Tiger hunting."

"On a Sunday? What's he trying to do? Catch one on its way to church?"

"Very funny. He'll have the last laugh if he actually catches one today."

Foetus coughed again. It looked like it hurt him. "You still don't get it, do you? He's not trying to catch one. The longer he spends looking, the longer he's getting paid by that rich Yank. The minute he finds one, bang, his livelihood is gone."

"That's not true. The reason Moose hasn't found a Tiger yet is he's been too busy training me."

"Bullshit. You and Moose have got more chance finding a ridgy-didge Tasmanian Aborigine."

"What are you talking about? Plenty of Aborigines live in Tasmania."

"Not black ones."

"Maybe they're not jet black but they've still got black blood."

"Bullshit. They've got red blood like you and me. What's more, most of 'em have got fair hair and blue eyes. I used to ride with a so-called Aborigine in the days when it wasn't trendy to be half-caste."

"You can't say that!"

"Why not? That's what we all called Bluey Brown. He had blue eyes and a carrot-red beard. He *was* half-caste."

Johnno felt increasingly uncomfortable with the conversation. "Has the doctor indicated how long you'll be in here?"

"Doctor? What doctor? Apparently someone will see me on his rounds tomorrow morning."

"No one's looked at you?"

"All I've seen today is a nurse sticking a thermometer in my gob every hour. And Big Bob."

Johnno looked at him quizzically.

Foetus unzipped his leather pants to reveal his cleanly shaven groin. "You should have seen the size of him. I am in no shape to argue."

A buzzer sounded, indicating visiting hours were over. As Johnno left the room, he passed a hefty woman who was wheeling a man with wet hair through the door.

"If it isn't the old cow herself?" muttered Foetus, loud enough to be heard.

Sister Rowbottom helped Bubby back into bed, then walked over to Foetus's bedside. "I've been giving it some thought and I've decided to offer you a compromise."

"Screw you, lady, it's a bit late for compromise."

"After mulling over it, I do see your point about you wanting to wear your leather jacket. But you must try to understand my point of view. The last thing I want is for a gang of bikies to come traipsing into my hospital. If you insist on wearing those leathers, we need to disguise you some other way."

"Disguise me? How?"

"How many people would recognise you without your beard?"

Foetus felt every one of his facial muscles flex. "I started growing this beard when I was 12," he gasped.

"That's settled then. I'll send Bob up with his scissors and razor. That way, you can keep your leather outfit."

FIVE

A PLACE OF MYSTERY AND POSSIBLY BEANS

JAMES WAS the latest in a long line of family mayors. Every mayor of Windy Mountain had been a descendant of Colonel Richard Northan who had founded the town in 1841.

Why he called the town what he did was a mystery. Perhaps he had eaten beans that day? But that didn't explain the 'mountain' bit. In sight were some rolling hills lightly populated with growing sub-divisions, but the only proper peak in sight was Bing Bong Mountain far in the distance.

Nobody knew why the main drag was called the High Street either. It was a flat, wide road flanked with oak trees, but the highest point was the old stone bridge that crossed the meandering Bing Bong River and poured visitors into the business district.

Colonel Northan planted the first Cox Orange Pippin apple trees on the outskirts of town in 1850.

His orchard had been passed down the family line until it came into James's hands in the early 1980s. That's when he started talking up the stories about the ghost, which were already part of local folklore. Sergeant Birtwistle didn't believe the stories, but Mayor Northan didn't care. Fanning those flames was much cheaper than hiring a security firm to keep people away. Few people wanted to trespass when they thought the ghost of Colonel Richard Northan might tie them to a tree and whip them with his cat'o'nine tails, just like he used to punish Irish convicts under his command.

When the orchard's manager retired in 1991, James decided to look to the export market rather than servicing local ventures. But when he discovered those old varieties of apples had become unfashionable with the big Japanese market, he decided to divest himself of the orchard all together. But that plan hadn't worked either. The For Sale sign had become rusty over the two years since.

Johnno had heard about the Brian Jacobs Memorial Commune in Gympie, and had decided he had much to contribute to the conserva-tionist cause.

He had hitched 1100 miles down to Melbourne and taken a deckchair crossing on the *Abel Tasman,* which brought him across Bass Strait.

He had hitch-hiked to within about a mile of Windy Mountain and walked the rest of the way. The town boundary sign said Welcome to *Windy Mountain, population 3003.* Had he entered from the other end of the town, that sign said Windy Mountain had 3004 people.

When Johnno walked into the centre he stopped right in front of a business called Tiger Kowalski's Dancing School, which was right across the road from the police station. With a backpack on his shoul-ders, and a map in his hands, he stood gawking at the signage.

"It's not really a dancing school," came a voice from over his shoulder.

Johnno turned around to see a man about his age. He was wearing a brown suit. "You look lost. Can I help you?"

Johnno dug into his pocket and pulled out a note, with the name of his prospective new home.

The man examined the address, and a look of puzzlement washed over his face. "The place you want is a bit out of town."

"Something wrong?"

"It's just . . . well, you don't look the type."

"I knew it. You could tell I am a Queenslander, right?"

"Are you?" The man's face brightened. "Why would you leave that sunshine to become a conservationist in damp old Tassie? I can't wait to get out of the place so I can work on one of the big newspapers on the mainland."

"You're a newspaper reporter?"

"Sure am." He extended his hand. "Norman J. Hit."

"Call me Johnno."

The reporter pointed to his right. "Blackstump Road is about a mile that way, turn left, you can't miss it."

It was only after Johnno had trudged up the road, he stopped and thought, "If it's not a dancing school what is it?" He turned and saw Norman J. Hit had headed off in the other direction and was well beyond shouting distance.

He turned again and continued towards the turn, which led him to the Brian Jacobs Memorial Commune.

Johnno got halfway through the application form before he realised he was never going to meet their requirements. But the woman was good about it. She suggested he might be better suited to the place next door, which was a commune in the loosest sense of the word.

SIX

I SURE WANT TO GET A LOOK AT THAT DADGUM CAT

MOOSE WAS glad to see the reds and yellows of the new day's sky as he stoked up the campfire to boil the billy.

He had tossed and turned in his sleeping-bag all night. He had never felt pressure like this! Who would have thought the weight of expectations from the football fans could become much heavier than the expectations of finding a Tasmanian Tiger, which authorities in 1986 had declared extinct.

As the season had progressed, more and more fans had crowded into the Windy Mountain Tigers' sheds at the end of games. More and more voices sang the victory song. More and more people had patted him on the back. He had heard them talk too: "Best player we've ever had. We can finally win the premiership with this bloke in the team."

Moose's fate was now in the hands of the tribunal, and he had no doubt he'd be found guilty. The umpire would have had to be blind to have not seen the punch from so close by!

If he was suspended, Moose couldn't play in the grand final. At his age he knew it would probably spell the end of his career.

Moose was 33. He grew up in Hobart with the first name of Bruce, and had excelled at both sporting and academic pursuits. He won a scholarship to study medicine at the University of Tasmania. But being in close confines with other people gave him panic attacks. Lecture halls and laboratories suffocated him. So he quit uni. For the next eight years he wandered the globe, taking whatever work he could find so he could save enough money to move on to the next destination.

Bruce was driving home from work in bumper-to-bumper traffic in Texas when the stretch limo in front of him stopped suddenly. Bruce's tyres squealed as he slammed on his brakes and he skidded into the back of the big black car.

He stood arguing with the chauffeur on the side of the road.

Bruce gulped when the passenger got out of the back seat. It was none other than millionaire philanthropist Tim Noah junior. He looked thinner than he looked on television, but he still had a middle-aged spread and was at least a head taller than the chauffeur, who he motioned to get back to his seat.

Noah wore cowboy boots, had a large hat on his head and chewed on a mighty big cigar. "I thought I recognised that dadgum accent?" Noah twanged. "Aussie, right?"

"I'm from Tasmania."

"TAS-mania!" Mr Noah slapped the sides of his thighs. "That's where the TAS-manian Tiger lives."

"I think it's extinct."

"I hear plenty of sightings have been RE-ported."

Within a week Bruce was winging his way back to Australia, with a brief to find Noah a mating pair of Tasmanian Tigers.

Bruce spent several weeks in Hobart looking through old newspapers, and reading books on the Tasmanian Tiger. This ferocious-looking marsupial had roamed the island state for more than 40,000 years, but it had taken less than 200 years for hunting and disease to wipe the species out. Bruce talked to a number of people who claimed to have seen the animal. He settled on Windy Mountain as his search base and set up home in the old Cameron farmhouse.

Hardly anyone knew about him for two years. Then came Foetus whose gang had deserted him at the Dancing School. Bruce offered Foetus shelter for the night — and he was still there three years later.

Two years after Foetus came, Lozza arrived. Then Johnno knocked on the door. Somewhere in between, the greenies moved in up the road.

Johnno was responsible for Bruce becoming known as Moose on a windswept late afternoon in May. Johnno said he had heard the local footy club was looking for new players and might pay them some money. Bruce would never forget the look on Johnno's face when he told Tiger Kowalski he played at flyhalf, only to be told, "We play real footy here, mate."

Johnno went all red. "You knew, Bruce, didn't you? You could have told me they didn't actually play rugby here!"

Bruce had grown up playing Aussie Rules, but he had not played since leaving school. He had been a beanpole as a teenager but now his body had bulked out to fill his 6 foot 6 inch skin.

He really couldn't have blamed the other Windy Mountain players on that first night questioning his footy credentials. Let's face it, not too many footballers had bushy beards and a ponytail. Heck, he didn't even have any boots.

"Are you sure you know what you are doing, mate?" Tiger shouted as Bruce ran on to the oval in his bare feet.

Twenty minutes later, the coach had no doubts.

Tiger called Bruce over and then summoned a player from the training track. This bloke wiped the sweat from his brow by lifting up his guernsey

Tiger pointed downwards. "I know Billy's not as big as you, Bruce. But look at the size of his feet."

He then turned to Billy. "I want you to lend Bruce your boots until he can get some of his own."

"But I've only got one pair of boots, coach."

Tiger growled back at him. "You really need to think about what's good for the team."

Bruce was offered a deal he couldn't refuse.

If Windy Mountain won the premiership, the club would send a working bee to paint the outside of the Cameron farmhouse. Tiger said he knew where he could get hold of as much paint as he needed, as long as Bruce wasn't fussy about the colour.

As the weeks passed Bruce became a star half-forward flanker/ruck-rover, and the fans nicknamed him Moose, while the man now known as Billy Gumboots warmed the bench in most games. Billy had the potential to seal a permanent place in the team but the selectors felt he lacked mobility in his alternative rubber boots. It didn't help they were bright blue and didn't match the Tigers' colours. Moose told himself Billy Gumboots had time on his side, being in his early 20s.

Moose was inspirational. Before long, Tiger stripped Brian Billson of the captaincy and gave it to Moose.

On the ground, nothing fazed him.

Off the ground was a different story, especially as the crowds began to build as the team became premiership contenders. Even midway into the season, sheepdogs often outnumbered the people in the crowd. But by spring, spectators came out like wattle blooms. Moose didn't know Windy Mountain had that many people.

Moose honestly believed the team could win without him. He had been tagged out of the last two games, anyway. He did finally break the tag to score the winning goal against Blue River in the preliminary final but he had barely got a grab in the second semifinal against Slutz Plains, and his team had been soundly beaten as a result.

Moose rolled up his sleeping bag, kicked dirt on the fire and started tramping home through the bush.

———

He had made plaster casts of a few fresh animal tracks which may or may not have belonged to a Tasmanian Tiger.

Moose had also found a long piece of dung which he believed was probably a Tiger dropping. But the test results were inconclusive. It was certainly big enough to come from an adult Thylacine, but it could have just as easily come from a wild dog. The problem was nobody really knew what the Tasmanian Tiger ate in the wild.

Until he and Foetus nicked the phone box from the High Street, Moose gave Tim Noah regular phone updates on his progress.

Now they just exchanged letters and Moose picked up his pay-cheque from the local post office every month.

"I sure am eager to get a look at that big cat," Noah wrote.

Moose didn't have the heart to tell him the Tasmanian Tiger wasn't actually a member of the cat family.

The early European settlers hadn't known what to make of it. The animal did look like a long *dog* with stripes. A fully grown Thylacine could weigh about 66 pounds and its powerful jaws could open 120 degrees. Yet it had a pouch and sometimes was seen hopping through the bush on its hind legs, using its heavy stiff tail for support. In 1830 the Van Diemen's Land Company introduced a Thylacine bounty and in 1888 Tasmania's parliament placed a price of £1 on the animal's head. Hunters cashed in big time with their snares or their guns. By the time the government scheme ended in 1909, 2184 bounties had been paid.

As Moose neared home, he made a decision. When he got to the farmhouse he was going to shave off his beard.

SEVEN
SAVED BY THE BAILIFF

RITA BIRTWISTLE WAS ABOUT to start ironing when one of the phones began ringing in the hallway. Even in the laundry, she could tell which phone it was. The red phone had a much louder, angrier ring than the black phone next to it.

She went to the back door and called out to her husband, who was in the garden.

"Randolph, the Mayor's ringing again."

"Answer it before he bursts a boiler, will you love? I'll be there in a sec."

Rita shook her head as she approached the phone and picked it up from the cradle. "He's coming, he's in the garden," she said, without giving the Mayor a chance to speak back. Then she let the receiver dangle and headed back down the hall to resume her ironing. Even above her footsteps on the wooden floorboards and amid the ticking of the grandfather clock in the hall, she could hear a flurry of invectives coming out of the earpiece.

She turned the iron to steam. If she had to listen to something hiss, at least it could do something practical. Why had Randolph ever agreed to having a direct line from the Mayor's office installed? Who did James Northan think he was anyway?

She heard Randolph take off his gumboots at the back door, then head to the hall. Now she could concentrate on starching shirts.

"Mr Mayor, how can I help you?" Birty said.

"Where have you been? The phone at the police station rang out, for goodness sake."

"Constable Smith must have been on another line. You should have tried again."

"Have you any idea how busy I am? Besides, why aren't you manning the station on a Monday morning? Isn't that what you are paid to do?"

"Fair go. I am entitled to some days off, you know?" Birty rubbed off some dried mud he saw on his fingernails. It reminded him that had the weather been nicer, he wouldn't even be having this conversation. He'd be fly-fishing. The Mayor hadn't worked out how to get a hotline installed on Bing Bong Mountain yet.

"You looked pretty relaxed to me when I saw you in church yesterday, sergeant."

Birty held the phone away from his ear and counted to 10 in his head. The Mayor was still ranting when he re-attached the phone to his ear, and he had to wait for him to stop for breath.

"You obviously didn't notice the bags under my eyes in church? Not only did I have to work to after midnight on Saturday, I had to get up for the early service so some bugger could release the prisoners. That bugger being me."

"Haven't you got juniors to delegate that kind of task to?"

"In theory, yes. In practice, both of them had rostered days off. Not a lot happens on Sunday and it means we can have extra manpower on other days. But someone has to release the prisoners."

"Why? I'd say it would teach them a lesson to stay locked up another night longer. It's not like they have seven years to serve any more, more's the pity."

Birty knew it was pointless trying to argue. "I've been pulling weeds out in the garden."

"At this time of the morning? Really? Weeding while Rome burns?"

"What's happened now?"

"You haven't heard about the drama at the hospital. A bikie caused all kinds of commotion when he was admitted on Saturday."

"And he's still causing trouble?"

"Daisy Rowbottom says he's quietened down. But she says no way can they release him while he's infectious."

"Good. So he'll still be in the ward tomorrow, which means I can check him out first thing."

"That might be too late, sergeant. He might have killed someone by then."

"Is that really likely?"

"Who knows? He's a bikie. I really think we should go and see him today."

"Today? But I told you, it's my day off . . ."

———

THE Little O sat in the spa taking in his new surroundings.

He could see the reflections of the editor and the chief-of-staff in the mirror on the ceiling. Thinning hair and man boobs. The walls were pink and there were blank video screens every direction he looked.

It was 8.30am. Riley O'Reilly (a.k.a. The Little O) was *The Pick Of The Crop's* football writer so he knew he had a long day ahead of him. But he couldn't wait to tell everyone what it was really like in here.

Dobber Leggs wasn't the only person in town who didn't know this place was actually a brothel. Sergeant Birtwistle didn't know either. Nor did The Mayor, which was the biggest surprise — because he secretly owned the place. For tax-minimisation purposes, Mayor Northan pretended not to own a lot of properties in the town. The difference with this one is he had also given Tiger Kowalski free rein to run the place as well as claiming he was the real owner. Mayor

Northan was happy to get that brown paper bag in the park each week.

How Tiger had kept Dobber Leggs at bay was masterly. It took hiding-in-plain-sight strategies to new heights.

Tiger had given him a complementary silver pass that entitled him to invite two colleagues to join him at 8am each weekday for the news-paper's morning editorial conference in one of the club's private rooms.

The conference laid the foundations for the following day's edition. Ideas for new and running stories were discussed, and goals and prior-ities were set.

Dobber Leggs and Reg Collins were regulars.

The third spot in the spa usually was filled by one of the young male reporters whom Dobber Leggs thought could benefit from the experience of seeing the editorial wheels being set in motion. Mostly it was Kevin Leggs, the editor's son; occasionally it was Peter Salter, the municipal roundsman; this particular day The Little O had finally got a guernsey. He felt privileged because in Dobber Leggs's eyes sport ran a long way behind local politics, law and order, and church fetes in importance.

The three men were dressed in their swimming togs — the editor and chief-of-staff in voluminous boardshorts, Riley O'Reilly in little red budgie smugglers. They sat on an underwater ledge around a table suspended over the spa from the ceiling. Later in the day this table served as a bar but Dobber Leggs used it as his desk. A copy of *The Pick of the Crop* was spread out before him as he went through it with a red marking pen, circling the many stories he thought the chief-of-staff should follow up.

Reg Collins and Riley O'Reilly sat silently on one side of the table as the editor deliberated on the other side.

Dobber Leggs's half-moon glasses were starting to steam up as he turned his head towards Riley O'Reilly and smiled. "You'd be amazed how many of this community's highest-ranking citizens come here each day, young fellow."

The editor locked eyes with his chief-of-staff, or he would have had he been able to see him. He removed his glasses and dipped them into the water in an attempt to un-steam them, then put them back on. "What's on the agenda today, Reginald?"

"I hear the greenies are up to something."

"Better get someone on to it then."

"That was the idea," the chief-of-staff muttered.

Whether the editor heard that, The Little O wasn't sure, but if he did he ignored it and kept charging on.

"How's that new chap I hired doing?"

"They tell me he's been down-table subbing for the past week or so while he becomes familiar with the paper."

"Whose idea was that?" The editor looked towards the ceiling. "The sooner he starts running things, the sooner he can whip our lame-brains into shape."

"Really? Well, if you're sure that's what you want, I'll talk to someone."

Sean McWhirter was in his mid-20s and his background in Sydney was as a down-table subeditor. But Dobber Leggs had recruited him as night editor. This meant as soon as the editor went home, he would have total control.

Dobber Leggs focused again on marking his newspaper. Without looking up, he said, "What's young Norman Hit assigned to today? Remember, he needs time for my special project."

"Once he's cleared police rounds and courts, I'd think he'll have loads of spare time. If recent lists are any guide, the most exciting case will be The Big O's usual Monday morning appearance."

The editor looked up at Riley O'Reilly with a puzzled look. "What have you done wrong?"

"No, not Riley," Reg Collins said. "He's The Little O."

"Who's The Big O then?"

"He's the town drunk, remember?"

Dobber Leggs looked even more puzzled. "I thought Whish-Willson was the town drunk."

"That was years ago. You must remember The Big O?" Reg Collins said. "He used to write our religion column. Now he writes our wine column."

Dobber Leggs ignored the look of disbelief and turned his attention again to Riley O'Reilly. "You know Windy Mountain has won through to the grand final? It's very big for the town."

Reg Collins took a deep breath. "He only covered the preliminary final," he mumbled again, this time more loudly.

Riley saw the editor look sideways at the chief-of-staff but before he could ask him what he had said, The Little O said, "Moose Routley got reported, sir."

"Who?" Dobber Leggs scrunched up his face. "Does anyone really care?"

Reg Collins came to the rescue. "Moose being reported is really quite a big deal. That's why I asked Riley to be here this morning. If Moose gets rubbed out, which seems likely, Windy Mountain will face an uphill battle to win on Saturday."

"How come I've never heard of him?"

Reg Collins shook his head. "We've tried to do stories on him several times and failed, remember? He's also looking for the Tasmanian Tiger."

"Oh, him? Our readers aren't interested in reading about hippies. They'll want to know about our Win-A-Cow competition though. How's that going, Reginald?"

"The response has slowed down."

"Really?" The editor scratched his head and sent flakes of dandruff drifting through the air. "When I was a young man, readers would have been queuing up outside the newspaper office in their thousands for a chance to win a cow. Which reminds me, Reginald, how are you going with the arrangements for the draw?"

"I'm still trying to finalise it but it's not looking good. I spoke to Oodles Noodle on the phone and he says no way will the Mayor let us take the cow on the ground at halftime."

"But did you tell him this is a *special* occasion?"

"I tried. But he said we'd have to make the draw outside the boundary line."

"That won't do. I want our readers at that game to see the cow during the draw. I don't care what you have to do; just see to it. OK?" He banged down a fist, spraying water everywhere.

———

JOHNNO propped his bike against a telegraph pole, and climbed the internal stairs that took him above the Wind Tunnel Cafe. He couldn't remember having been up this early on a Monday morning but he had to see the lawyer the Big O had recommended to him.

A sign on the door at the top of the stairs said to knock and enter, but when he entered someone nearly took his eye out with the slide of a trombone.

The shocked musician put the instrument down on the table in front of him, and stood up. He was tall and skinny.

Johnno held a hand over his eye. No contact had actually been made but it was a reflex action. "Sorry. I was looking for a lawyer called Terry Mason."

The chin-less trombonist gave a little bow. "At your service."

"You don't look like a lawyer!"

"I was practising for the halftime entertainment at the grand final." Mason looked for some sign he had been recognised, then said, "I'm first trombone in the Windy Mountain Brass Band."

"Ryan O'Shannessy recommended you."

"Did he?" Mason's eyes gleamed. "Good old Father O'Shannessy used to be my parish priest."

"And you represent him?"

Mason shook his head. "I have so few clients these days, I'm sure I'd remember."

"Really!" Johnno pinched the bridge of his nose. "I'm due to front the magistrates court at 2pm, so I haven't got much time to shop around."

"You'd better sit down then." Mason walked two steps over to a desk in another corner of the tiny room, and Johnno sat down on the other side. "What do you mean by *shop around*?"

"Find another lawyer."

"Oh? Not much call for another lawyer in this town." Mason blew air from his cheeks. "The good news is I have the potential to be quite good, given a bit of practice. In fact, I'd say, if I had even half the amount of time practising the law as I do practising my trombone . . . "

Johnno folded his arms.

The lawyer frowned. "I assume Father O'Shannessy did tell you I haven't actually won a case for years?"

Johnno must have looked as pale as he felt, because Mason brightened. "I wouldn't let that worry you though, old chap. It increases the odds I'll win the next one."

Johnno ran his fingers through his hair. "Look, I came here in the hope you could sort me out. I've never even been in a court room."

"Why don't you tell me the story from the beginning and let me plan your defence?"

So Johnno did.

After he had finished, the lawyer smiled at him. "My advice is you plead guilty, and only speak when you're spoken to. Just try not to get overawed by the surroundings that you'll probably find confusing. I'll present a case of mitigation."

"But I've already told you I didn't even know I was committing a crime."

"Oh dear boy, ignorance is no grounds for innocence. Whether you knew it or not, you did break the law. But don't worry, Mr Rockingham isn't what we call in the business a hanging judge. When I'm finished painting you as such a good citizen it wouldn't surprise me if he lets you off on a good behaviour bond."

This made Johnno feel a whole lot better.

"It's best to let me do most of the talking. If Mr Rockingham asks you to say anything, keep it short and polite. Address him by the title

Your Worship; not Your Honour. That's a mistake a lot of people make."

———

ALL he saw from the corner of his eye was a flash of purple as someone sat down beside him on the wooden bench outside Court No. 1. When the bench wobbled, he looked sideways and came face to face with a peroxide blonde in a lurid leisure suit.

"What are you looking at?" She fired a blast of stale cigarette breath at Johnno.

"Sorry. It was a reflex action."

"My boyfriend doesn't like other blokes hitting on me."

"I wasn't—"

"You're just lucky he's not here."

"Shouldn't he be supporting you?"

"That's a laugh. I'm here to support *him*." She sniffed loudly. "I don't know why they don't let him sit here with us instead of making him sit in that cell in the basement? They reckon he's violent, but he hasn't got a violent bone in his body. If he ever gets out of those hand-cuffs, I reckon he'll kill the next fucking person who says he's violent."

At this, Johnno turned and looked ahead at the opposite wall. It was hard to get the vision of the woman with the three chins out of his mind. This wasn't helped by the fact he could smell her cheap perfume and hear her raspy intakes of breath. It was 1.45pm, and the court was due to start in 15 minutes.

He had arrived early.

From the road, the sign on the awning of the grand white sand-stone building announced it was the Courthouse, built in 1842. But the building's chief use these days was as the local council chambers. Rooms once occupied by various court officials now housed council officers and the Mayor, and what used to be used as the actual court-room upstairs was now used to convene the weekly meeting of coun-cillors every Tuesday night.

But the council also hired out the venue every second Monday so it could host the Windy Mountain Magistrate's Court.

Johnno had found his name on a list pinned to a noticeboard in the foyer downstairs, and it had directed him up here.

He was the first one. Then a bubble-gum chomping teenager came up the stairs with a young mother and her toddler in tow, and they sat together on an adjoining bench. Three more young strangers arrived together, and they sat down on a bench a bit further along. Then Purple Leisure Suit arrived and sat in a space that ought to have seated one more person. This wasn't a problem until a latecomer staggered up the stairs. He was clearly under the influence of something. He stopped and looked around until his addled gaze fell on Johnno's bench. He stared as he swayed. He was wearing a tatty sleeveless denim jacket, had tattoos on his biceps, and hadn't shaved.

"Why don't you move your fat arse?" he finally said.

Johnno heard Purple Leisure Suit sniff again. "Who's going to make me? You?" Out of the corner of his eye, he saw her raise an index finger. "You don't recognise me, do you? I'm Rollo's better half?"

Next to arrive was Father O'Shannessy. Johnno nodded towards him as he paced up and down. One more man arrived, and he found a wall to slump against. By this time, Staggering Man was sitting on the tiled floor, his back against the same wall.

The first person was called on the stroke of 2pm. Johnno was the only one left when Purple Leisure Suit came storming out. She looked at him as if he were prey. "I'm not wasting the best years of my life while he's inside for three years. You looking for a girlfriend?"

Johnno was mightily relieved when a bailiff stuck his neck out of the doorway and called him. He was directed to a small wood-panelled box at the front of the court, a few yards away from a man in a black gown.

"Are you Leslie John Johnson?" he asked.

"I am, Your Worship." Johnno bowed.

"I am not His Worship." The man nodded towards the raised plat-form. "I'm the clerk of the court."

The clerk continued, "Leslie John Johnson, you are charged with, on or about September 12, on a public road in the State of Tasmania, namely the High Street in Windy Mountain, you did commit a crime, namely that you did appear in public, between the hours of sunset and sunrise, dressed in female attire, namely a pink dress and green stockings, with a Red Delicious apple and a Golden Delicious apple stuffed down the respective cups of a brassiere, which was attached to your person. How do you plead?"

Terry Mason, who was sitting at the big table behind Johnno, sprang to his feet.

"If it pleases Your Worship. I appear for this defendant. He has instructed me to enter a plea of guilty but there are mitigating circumstances."

As the legal talk began, Johnno looked around the plush surroundings. He was still annoyed about having to plead guilty but he was heartened by Mason's reassurances. Besides, it was out of his control now. He had no choice but to let the lawyer go into bat for him. Mason stood at the table opposite a thick-set police prosecutor. At the back of the room were three rows of bench seats where Junior Constable Stretch and Constable Smith sat. At one side of the room was a long bench with a hooded desktop. He knew it was a press box because he recognised the occupant who had directed him that first day. Did Norman J. Hit have coconut trees on all his ties?

Johnno's mind-wandering was interrupted by the bang of the magistrate's gavel. "Mr Johnson, are you listening to me?"

"Oh, um, yes . . ." Johnno hadn't actually absorbed a word of the proceedings.

"Do you understand what the sentence implies?" The magistrate exhaled. "It means you will devote 82 hours of your time doing community work."

Johnno looked towards Mason but the lawyer wouldn't make eye contact. Johnno turned back to the magistrate.

"Is that clear, Mr Johnson?" Mr Rockingham said.

"Er, um . . . yes." Johnno bowed his head.

"Yes, what?"

"Yes, Your Majesty."

———————

DILLY BROWN stopped suddenly. "This is pointless," she said, as her three colleagues in the tight circle behind her stopped, too, to avoid a pile-up.

Dilly was carrying an old broomstick with a placard stapled to the top and it was slumped over her shoulder.

"This is the stupidest protest I've been in."

The greenies had been picketing their own front yard at the Brian Jacobs Memorial Commune for seven hours now. They had started at 8am, stopped for lunch about 1pm, and pushed on after their lentil stew. Only three people had passed by all day. Johnno had ridden past on his bike earlier this morning, and Moose and Lozza had stopped and enquired what this protest was all about.

Dilly almost spat into William Archibald-Smith's face. "Did you hear what that Tasmanian Tiger hunter said? He said they were on their way to visit the bikie in hospital. That means unless someone wanders lost on to Blackstump Road, no one is left we can try to convert."

The greenies all had signs. John Nitram's read, *Save the Green Swift Parrot Before it's Too Late*. William's said, *Please Don't Let Them Become Extinct*. Sarah Sarandon had recycled her sign from a past protest. It said, *Let the Orchard Run Free*.

"Can't you hold your sign up properly, Dilly," William said. "I can't even see what it says."

She looked skywards, then lifted the sign up. It said, "*Who Cares Wins?*"

"Do you know what they'll calling us in town?" Dilly glared. "Well, do you? They reckon we're the Greenies Lite or the Light Greenies. And is it any wonder?"

"What? You don't think they'd commend us for the responsible nature of our protest?" William said. "Staying out of harm's way? Keeping the wheels of commerce going by not impeding workers from doing their jobs?"

"Actually, I think we've become a laughing stock," Dilly said. "If we simply have to lobby for the welfare of your beloved Green Swift Parrot wouldn't it make more sense to form a picket line somewhere we'd actually be seen?"

John's sign slumped to right angles to the ground. "She has a point, man."

William hurled his sign to the ground. They all watched it bounce, sending little droplets of water into the air. "I don't believe you people. We put this to the vote, and this is what we decided as a group. What's changed?"

"I voted against it," Dilly said.

"You still voted," William said. "We all voted to hold a peaceful protest against the mindless destruction of one of our rare birds. It was three against one. What don't you understand about majority rules?"

Dilly moved closer so her nose nearly touched William's nose. "It's a given Sarah always votes for you. But the reason John voted with you is you wore him down, like you usually do."

William smiled. "I prefer to think he finally listened to sense." He turned to John. "That right, mate?"

"Whatever you say, man."

Now Dilly slammed her sign into a small puddle.

Sarah and John stepped back to avoid the splash, but William was too slow to react and he copped the worst of the splatter on his lower legs. He looked down at his mud-splattered jeans and grimaced.

"Why did you have to do that?"

"Serves you right for holding the picket here," Dilly said.

William bent down and tried to brush the worst of the mud away. When he rose, he waved his finger at Dilly. "It's not my fault you can't be more persuasive with your arguments."

"But it *is* your fault we're walking around in this silly little circle for a protest no one will ever see," Dilly said.

"I've got broken fingernails," Sarah moaned.

Dilly glared at Sarah. "You've always got broken finger nails." She gestured towards William. "It's a wonder you don't break more fingernails with the amount of laundry and dishes you wash for him." Then she pointed to Sarah's footwear. "And whoever heard of protesting in high heels?"

"You leave Sarah out of this," William said. "You were the one who complained first."

"Yes," Sarah said. "You think this protest is tough? You should have been with us and Brian at the Franklin."

"I never complained about the hardships involved with this protest," Dilly said. "My gripe is with this protest full stop. It's stupid. It's a waste of time."

"Don't you care about the fate of the Green Swift Parrot?" asked Sarah.

"I think our valuable time would be better spent tackling more important issues."

"Like what?" asked William.

"Like, for one, the heritage of the Tasmanian Aborigine," Dilly said.

"What?" John said.

"The Tasmanian Koori," Dilly said.

"What have Aborigines got to do with conservation?" William said. "We're trying to save the Green Swift Parrot."

"Aren't people worth saving too?"

"The people aren't in any danger, are they?" Sarah asked.

"The Tasmanian Aborigines are under threat," Dilly said, as she launched herself into a well-rehearsed speech. "When white man invaded our island in the 18th century we numbered 8000. We had lived in peace for 20,000 years. We had no wars, no disease; life was perfect. But in less than 100 years we were hunted and killed by your white ancestors and cut down by European diseases. The last few survivors were rounded up and expelled from our homeland. When the last full-blooded Tasmanian Aborigine died in 1888, a whole race was eradicated."

"*You* look pretty white to me," William said.

"That's racist," Dilly said.

"No, it's not," William said. "It's an observation. I think the people you label as our white ancestors are probably just as much *your* white ancestors. If you've got any black body parts you keep them covered up pretty well."

Dilly's eyes started welling up. "You're so insensitive. You don't know how hard it is being an Aborigine?"

Dilly produced a handkerchief from the top pocket of her overalls, wiped away some tears and blew her nose. John and Sarah stood looking at their feet.

John spoke softly. "I'm starting to have second thoughts about this whole scene, man. Dilly might be right. Perhaps we are wasting our time?"

"What kind of attitude is that for a conservationist?" William said.

"It's the kind of attitude that comes from walking around in a circle for five hours with a placard hardly anyone will ever see," John said. "I'm becoming disillusioned, man."

William's frown deepened. "But what about the Green Swift Parrot?"

"I don't even know what they look like. I've never seen one," John said.

"And you never will unless we save them," William said.

"Maybe they've gone already?" Sarah said.

"That's nonsense," William said. "They've been seen nesting in Northan's apple orchard. But every time an apple is picked, their little nests are in danger of being toppled from their perches. It's up to us to save them. What could be more important? What more do you all want?"

"Oh, I don't know . . ." John said, ". . . a normal life, perhaps?"

"What?" Even William's bobbing Adam's apple looked red.

"You know?" John said. ". . . a job, a proper home . . .?"

"You've got a home here with us," Sarah said.

"And we've all got a job to do," William said.

"The pay's lousy, man," John said. "I've got three university degrees and all I get each week is the same dole cheque they give to everyone else. I think I deserve more."

"That's a very relevant point." Sarah had majored in journalism and communications. "We've all got our university degrees to worry about."

"Great!" William said. "After we block the building of pulp mills and save the forests, the wild rivers, and save the Green Swift Parrot and the Tasmanian Aborigine, we can start chaining ourselves to Social Security offices. Maybe we could declare the dole a National Heritage Area."

Dilly's tears had gone now. "I think we should put this protest to another vote," she said.

———

AS MOOSE and Lozza went in through the revolving door, they passed by the two officials leaving the hospital on the other side. They couldn't miss them when they were dressed like that.

"Must be someone important in the hospital," Lozza said after the door deposited them out into a carpeted area.

Moose looked very official himself in his suit, and he led the way over to the reception desk. He coughed to try to get the attention of the receptionist who was standing looking out the window. But she was preoccupied watching the VIP visitors disappear down the front steps. One wore a neat uniform complete with stripes, shiny medals and a cap. The other was dressed in a blue pin-stripe suit and wore gold chains around his neck.

She jumped a little when she turned and saw someone was there.

"Where can I find Gus Foot?" Moose asked.

Lozza looked sideways at him. He glared back at her. "He does have a real name, you know? Did you think his mum christened him Foetus?"

Moose ran his hand along the smooth counter as the receptionist thumbed through the registry cards, her frown deepening as she went.

"Try *Foetus*," Lozza said.

The receptionist's face brightened when she found the registration. "Why didn't you say? He insisted on going into our records as Foetus."

Lozza flashed a phoney smile. "He's such a funny bloke."

"Popular, too," the receptionist said. "You're the second lot of visitors in quick succession."

Moose glanced at Lozza who looked just as perplexed. Maybe Johnno had been in again? Why then hadn't he mentioned it? They had run into him near the courthouse. He did seem to be in a bit of a headspin after his court appearance though.

They found Foetus looking miserable in Room 15. Despite being still lathered in sweat, he was sitting on the side of his bed wearing a starched white hospital gown.

He brightened when he looked up. "Well, look at you! You think wearing a suit is going to protect you Moose?"

"Protect me from what exactly?"

"Me. You have no idea how awful this place is! And it's your fault I'm here."

"I did what a mate had to do. How was I to know you'd just make it worse by trying to escape?"

Foetus pouted again.

"For your information, this suit comes from Tiger." Moose ran a hand down one of his sleeves. It was soft and silky. "He hired it because he wants me to look the best for the tribunal tonight."

"You worked out your story?"

"I'm going for the George Washington defence. *He* admitted chopping down the cherry tree, *I'm* going to admit I jobbed that bloke."

"What's got into you?" Foetus looked horrified. "No one ever got off anything by pleading guilty."

"Yeah, well I can't see the point in trying to fight the inevitable this time. The umpire saw me do it." Moose tugged at Foetus's gown.

"Anyway, you're not looking too shabby yourself." He recoiled. "Yuk, it's saturated with sweat. Shouldn't you be in bed?"

Foetus grunted. "You sound like *her*. It was either wear this or lose my beard. And nobody's touching my beard!" Foetus pulled a face. "The old cow better not feel too happy with herself though because it's not over yet, not by a long way."

He stood up and hopped over to the window.

"You know your backside is showing?" Lozza called after him.

Then she covered her mouth with a hand when she saw Foetus was opening the double-doors to the balcony, and she twigged what he was about to do.

Foetus turned around and flashed a mischievous smile. He grabbed the sides of his gown and held them apart.

Outside, people were probably oblivious as they went about their business. Their attention would probably focus on the black and yellow displays in shop windows but there was always a slight chance some poor sod would look up.

Moose laughed. "So you're still causing a commotion, I see."

After a couple of minutes, Foetus hopped back to his bed and sat down on the side. "How did Johnno get on in court?"

"He got 82 hours of work orders," Lozza said.

"Eighty-two hours!" Foetus's voice rose. "Is that all? He should have been shackled to a balls and chains, the little pervert."

Moose shook his head. "Do you know when you're getting out?"

"That's what the mare and the pig wanted to know too."

Lozza frowned. Moose frowned.

"Mayor Northan and Sergeant Birtwistle," Foetus said. "They were just here."

"So that's who those dorks were?" Moose said. "What did they want with you?"

"They told me they don't like bikers, and suggested I move on to someone else's town."

Foetus looked behind him to make sure no one else had entered the room. Bubby had gone for yet another bath. Foetus lowered his voice. "I reckon you could make some money around here, Moose."

"Keep talking."

"It's a twist on the bushrangers' whiskers caper."

"In here?"

"Shhh! Keep it down, will you." Foetus waved his hands. "I didn't say *exactly* like the whiskers caper, I said it was a twist." Then he smiled his tooth-challenged smile again. "Has anyone told you how much you look like a doctor dressed in that suit?"

Foetus turned to Lozza. "How's your Repetitive Strain Injury, honey?"

She grimaced. "My right wrist is still killing me."

"How's your left wrist?"

"Fine. Why?"

Foetus motioned for Moose to lean in closer, and he whispered in his ear.

————

MAYOR NORTHAN and Birty stood on the footpath alongside the policeman's station wagon, which looked more grey than blue as daylight faded.

"How long did he say he has lived in Blackstump Road?" The Mayor's chains of office jangled as his voice trembled.

Birty scratched his head. "I've never seen him in town. Have you?"

"Really sergeant! It's not my job to notice these things, it's *yours*. I hope your successor keeps a better eye on the goings-on in this town than you."

"That's not fair! I'd say the crime rate in this town is close to zero. wouldn't you?"

"No, I wouldn't." He fixed his death stare on the policeman. "For starters, what about the missing phone box? You seem to have no idea what's become of that."

Birty gave the glimpse of a smile. "Everyone is allowed one missing phone box in a long career." His grin broadened. "Anyway, I hear phone boxes are being phased out. That makes Windy Mountain a trendsetter."

"Don't be flippant with me, sergeant." Mayor Northan jangled again. "My observation is you've become less vigilant the nearer you've approached retirement."

Birty's smile lines disappeared. "You do know that, technically speaking, Blackstump Road is outside the town's limits."

"Don't try to hide behind technicalities, sergeant. You know as well as I do that whatever he gets up to out there is most probably illegal, which damages the reputation of Windy Mountain."

Birty dug out his car keys. "Sure you don't want a lift?"

"No thanks, sergeant. I don't think I can trust you to get me safely home."

The truth was the Mayor had some things to tidy up back at his office. But it wouldn't hurt to reinforce the message he thought the policeman had become old and doddery, and incompetent.

"Please yourself." Birty headed to the other side of the car, shaking his head and muttering. He slammed the door behind him and the engine revved into life.

Mayor Northan watched Birty drive off in a puff of smoke, then began strolling towards the council chambers.

He had mixed thoughts about the Tigers making the footy grand final. He wasn't looking forward to shaking the hands of those Neanderthals and trying to get them to say something half-literate, but he had to admit this whole occasion was good for commerce.

The whole town seemed to be dressed up in the club's colours. Most of the shops had grand final displays in their windows, and black and yellow signs were everywhere.

Mayor Northan nodded contentedly to himself. It was good for business, all right. And if Windy Mountain managed finally to win the premiership, the commercial spinoffs would be even better.

He looked upwards to admire the bunting strung above the street. What the … ?

———

WISH-WASH spun around and saw them as they came over the brow of a small hill. They whizzed past the street light in a blur of chrome and black leather. Wish-Wash counted 20 motorbikes as they sped towards the town centre.

Foetus was sitting on his bed when he heard them, and the familiar noise filled him with hope. With Moose and Lozza off doing their bogus rounds of the hospital, he hopped over to the window again and looked out. They were bikers, all right. What he didn't know was: who they were?

Mayor Northan stood rubbing his eyes in disbelief. It had taken him 15 minutes to get over the shock of seeing that bare bottom, now his shaking made him jingle and jangle again as the bikies slowed down 50 yards from The Applecart and pulled up right outside the glow coming from the pub windows.

Those bikers who had helmets removed them and hung them on their machines. Most of the men had long greasy hair, some tied in ponytails, and unkempt beards of varying lengths. They wore dirty blue jeans and leather jackets, which were emblazoned on the back with a picture of a feathered beast.

When the bikers filed through the front door, the regulars went scurrying out the back. The biggest, meanest-looking bikie approached the bar. Artie Rogerson gulped. He had seen shorter oak trees, and the ponytail and a black bandana made this bloke look more sinister.

"I'll have 16 beers, nine orange juices, and one scotch and coke," the bikie growled.

"Sorry, we don't have any of that." Reg was glad now his regulars were no longer there to hear the tremor in his voice. He normally prided himself on being the voice of authority in this place.

"You're kidding me?" The bikie looked left and right. "This looks like a pub to me."

"It is, but we only serve apple cider. It's double strength, we brew it ourselves."

The bikie smiled. He had two missing front teeth. "Why didn't you say? Give us 16, no, 17 ciders then. What about the orange juices?"

"Best I can do is apple juice," Rog said.

As Rog got to work behind the bar he saw the bikie remove his jacket, which he slung over the back of a chair on a nearby table. His T-shirt was adorned on the back with a red, black and yellow flag.

Rog nearly dropped a glass when the bikie turned and he saw the size of the man's tattooed arms.

"What are *you* looking at?"

"I was admiring the Aboriginal flag on your T-shirt," Rog lied.

"Really? You haven't seen one before?"

"Most of them have been up flagpoles."

The bikie looked around at his comrades, then cracked his knuckles. "That's where you might end up if you don't get a hurry-on with those drinks." The others laughed.

Some of the bikers were already on to their second ciders when Wish-Wash finally arrived from the outskirts of town. The jukebox in the corner was cranking out another *Shaddup Your Face* song. But when he looked around, he saw only large strangers.

His eyes finally locked on to those of Rog's, who looked glad to see him, which was a change on days like these he turned up in the much-ridiculed orange trousers he had picked up cheaply at a State Emergency Services fire sale.

The barman pointed to the stool he had relinquished to his replacement as town drunk, and now resided with The Big O's backside. "Wish-Wash, glad you could make it. Sit down, mate." He started pouring him a cider. "Drinks are on the house."

Wish-Wash started drinking slowly as he looked around and got the feel of his old seat. His confidence returned with every gulp.

Three glasses later, he had drawn around him a number of bikers.

Cider in hand, he captivated them with tales of apple pies, Windy Mountain's own resident bikie and, of course, the Tasmanian Tiger.

———

WHEN Moose climbed the stairs he was surprised to find Tiger Kowalski talking to Fred Stevens on the deck. Stevens was the field umpire who had reported him, and Tiger was there at the tribunal to represent him. It didn't seem right they were talking like old friends.

"Can I have a word, coach?" Moose pointed to a quiet corner.

"Certainly." Tiger followed him over.

Moose looked around to make sure no one could hear, and lowered his voice. "What's going on?"

Tiger brushed Moose's shoulder. "Told you you'd look the part in a nice suit."

"Don't *nice* suit me," Moose hissed. "What are you up to?"

"What makes you think I'm up to anything?"

"*You* talking to *him*, for starters."

"If you let me get a word in, I'll explain. Fred tells me he's decided to withdraw the report because he didn't actually see anything."

"He what?" Moose's eyes widened. "He was a few yards away from me!"

"Now he thinks about it, he says he might have been as far as 50 yards away."

Moose felt his heart skip a beat as the penny dropped. "You've paid him off?"

"Nothing of the sort. It came as a surprise to me, too. I only started talking to him because I thought I should do the decent thing and congratulate him. You know he's been selected to officiate in the grand final?"

Moose shook his head slowly from side to side. "I came here tonight thinking I didn't have a chance in hell of getting off and you're telling me . . ."

Tiger made a shhh sign with his finger. "Keep your voice down, will you? You want the journos to hear? They'd have a field day writing about dissension in the ranks." He squeezed Moose's shoulder. "Relax. didn't I tell you everything would be OK? I suppose it's good you look agitated though. The media likes a touch of the dramatic."

Moose gripped more tightly the plastic shopping bag he was carrying, causing it to rustle.

"What's in the bag?"

"Oh this?" Moose looked downwards. "I've come from the hospital. It's my housemate's dirty underwear. Take a look if you don't believe me?"

"Sheesh! Of course I don't want to see it, and nor will anyone else. Can't you put it down somewhere? I wouldn't have paid for that suit if I didn't think image was important. Some fashion accessory!"

"What happens now?"

"We go inside, Blind Freddy drops the charges and it'll be over in a matter of minutes. No doubt the press will then want to talk to you. Tell them how relieved you are, and how much you are looking forward to playing in the grand final."

Moose groaned. "You know how I hate speaking to the press!"

Tiger put a hand on Moose's shoulder again.

"Look, this goes with the territory. All you have to do is give them a couple of quick comments. Just make sure your halo is on straight for the cameras, and look relieved."

———

ONE HOUR passed. Two hours passed. Three hours passed. Still the bikers were holed up in The Applecart with Wish-Wash and Artie Rogerson.

News travelled quickly in Windy Mountain and it got more dramatic with every version told. Before long, many of the townsfolk believed Rog and Wish-Wash were being held hostage.

The first phone calls didn't start hitting the newspaper until about 7pm. By this time the editor and the chief-of-staff had gone home, leaving McWhirter in charge for the first time.

Coming from Sydney, where crime was more commonplace, McWhirter decided not to act straight away. "Let's monitor it," he told his staff, who were amazed with this new calmness.

But McWhirter's hand was forced by the weight of phone calls, some from townsfolk wondering if the time had come for Windy Mountain to be evacuated.

At 10pm he walked over to where Norman J. Hit was tapping away at a typewriter.

"What are you working on?" McWhirter peered over his shoulder.

Norman stopped and turned around. "It's an obituary."

"Really? No one told me anyone had died."

"That's because he hasn't yet. The word though is Gordon Rogers is on his last legs."

"But he's not actually dead?" McWhirter said it slowly.

"Mr Leggs asked me to get the obit ready just in case."

"I think this can wait until he at least stops breathing, don't you? I need you to get over to The Applecart and find out what's going on."

———

DILLY BROWN wasn't the only one who was yawning. The four conservationists sat around the kitchen table in varying degrees of fatigue. They had spent most of their daylight hours picketing, and now they were trying to come to a consensus about what to do next. They couldn't agree on anything. Every vote resulted in a 2-2 deadlock.

Dilly glanced at her watch, which told her it was nearly midnight. She knew what William Archibald-Smith's tactics were. He never ventured from his winning formula. Being the most boring person in the room, he really believed he could outlast everyone else to the point they'd agree to anything he suggested just so they could go to bed. He knew he could always count on Sarah's vote and sooner or later John Nitram would cave in.

The signs were looking good for him too. John Nitram's head was now nestled in his arms, which were folded on the table. He would start snoring at any moment.

This made what happened next even more surprising.

He lifted his head and said, "Sorry. How long have I been asleep?"

"Couldn't have been more than a few seconds," Dilly said.

"That's weird. I could have sworn I had a long dream about the Tasmanian Tiger." He came awake with new vigour. "Maybe we ought to be trying to save the Tiger rather than the Green Swift Parrot?"

William shook his head slowly from side to side. "It's too late, mate. The Tasmanian Tiger is already extinct. Can't we stick to the motion?"

"What *is* the motion?" Sarah was yawning like the person in class who just couldn't keep track any more.

William adjusted his beanie. "Whether or not we should have the Green Swift Parrot protest here or outside the council chambers in town."

Dilly Brown glared at him. "Haven't you heard a word we've said? We don't want to protest about a bird at all."

"I don't mind." Sarah examined her hands. "I'm just sick of these broken nails."

"Will you shut up about your broken nails," William said. "Nobody cares!"

Dilly saw the rage rise in Sarah's face. This was a turn up. William was normally so measured, inching ahead with well-chosen words, boring everyone stupid but seldom retreating and never faltering.

Dilly knew this was a rare opportunity to strike. "I'd like to move a new motion we abandon this silly protest and put our endeavours to better use in the name of conservation," she said quickly.

"I wondered how long it would take you to raise the topic of Aborigines!"

"That's where you're wrong." Dilly glared at him. "This has little to do with Aborigines. I can think of plenty of other constructive things we can do."

John spoke again. "I'll second the motion, Dilly, if you'll second my amendment."

William turned abruptly to John who was sitting next to Dilly on one side of the table. "What are you talking about? You haven't even *framed* an amendment!"

"I haven't had a chance, man; not with all this bickering."

"I thought you wanted to quit, and go and get a highly paid job?"

"I've changed my mind, man. I've decided to try to save the Tasmanian Tiger instead of the Green Swift Parrot. That's my amendment."

Quick as a flash, Dilly said, "I second that."

William smiled smugly at Dilly. "Even you're not stupid enough to believe we can do anything to bring back an extinct animal."

"It's no less stupid than holding a protest in our own front yard."

"You're doing this out of spite for me."

"No, I'm not," Dilly said. "Aborigines hold the Tasmanian Tiger very near and dear."

William still looked like he thought he had the upper hand, with Sarah's vote in the bag and his tried-and-tested ability to wear John down again.

But Dilly knew from the look on Sarah's face for a short time the momentum had swung.

She tried to press her advantage. "If the white man hadn't come to Tasmania, the Tasmanian Tiger would still sleep on our back porches."

"What porches?" William was laughing now. "Tasmanian Aborigines didn't even have proper houses."

John rubbed his eyes, "Will you guys stop arguing? Can't we just vote on the motion and amendment, and then open a discussion about what we can do to save the Tasmanian Tiger?"

"John, mate, the Tasmanian Tiger is extinct," William said slowly and deliberately. "Do I need to spell it out? It's D.E.A.D."

"That's not what Wish-Wash told us." Sarah was wide awake now.

"Who believes Wish-Wash!" William said. "Everyone knows he's careless with the truth."

"I believed him, man," John said. "They say he could have gone on to become a Rhodes scholar if he had wanted to follow the academic path."

"I believed him too," Sarah said.

"Me, too," Dilly said. It was a lie but what the heck?

"I don't believe this?" William looked from face to face and it dawned on him what was happening. His face went white. "For goodness sake, the man is the town drunk."

"*Former* town drunk," John said.

"He was drunk the night he says he saw a Tasmanian Tiger."

"You can't blame him for that," John said. "It was his job, man."

"Not only did he say he *saw* the Tasmanian Tiger, he says he *patted* it!" William said. "You believe that too?"

They voted first on Dilly's motion. It was carried three-one.

Then they voted on John's amendment. It was also carried three-one.

The next thing to decide was what form their Save The Tasmanian Tiger protest should take.

William made a show of looking at his watch.

"It's getting late. Maybe we should sleep on it?" He looked at Sarah. "Time for bed? We can resume our discussions in the morning."

Sarah tossed back her long hair. "Fine with me. I'll start drafting a press release." She locked eyes with William. "I don't know how long I'll be, but I'm sleeping in the spare room anyway so it will give you some quality time alone with that appendage you call Mr Happy."

EIGHT
THE GREAT SPERM ROBBERY AND OTHER TABLOID STORIES

TUESDAY'S EDITION of *The Pick Of The Crop* carried three cracking stories, which was unusual for a newspaper that was so often full of grey slabs of type that was probably of interest only to Dobber Leggs and six other people.

The headline on Page One screamed out,

The Great Sperm
Robbery at hospital

The Page Three headline said,

Muttonbirds deny siege, say
they are just misunderstood

And the Back Page said,

Star Tiger free to play in grand
final after umpire drops

charge

For the first time, the newspaper sold out before lunchtime.

————

JAMES Northan rarely bothered to read the local newspaper, even though he received a complementary copy each day. He always read *The Financial Review* from cover to cover. But *The Pick Of The Crop* seldom had anything in it he needed to read. Prue said it had a good crossword though, so he left it for his wife to pick up from the front lawn each day.

This was why he was unprepared for what he heard when he stormed into the police station shortly after 8am. He wanted to know what Sergeant Birtwistle was doing about the arrival of the bikers.

"Sorry, I don't have time to worry about them, Mr Mayor." Birty turned his back as he shuffled through a filing cabinet in search of records of known criminals in the district. "I'm up to my neck in semen."

Mayor Northan wondered if he had heard this correctly. He was standing on the other side of the counter looking at the sergeant's back. "But boats don't come this far up the river?"

Birty was shaking his head when he turned around. "I don't mean sailor seamen." He pointed towards his groin. "I mean semen semen."

Mayor Northan felt a vein in his neck pop up. He stared in disbelief.

"I haven't got time to explain." Birty reached behind him and slammed the drawer shut. "I can't tell you any more than was printed in the newspaper."

"What newspaper?"

"*The Pick Of The Crop* ran a story this morning."

"You can't be serious! Why would you believe anything that rag says?" Mayor Northan stamped his foot. "You have a sworn duty to brief me on what's happening."

Birty approached the counter, stooping over it until he was nearly face to face with the Mayor. "This is confidential, all right?" He rapped his large right index finger on the desk.

"Of course. I take the Official Secrets Act very seriously. But I might say you've got into a very bad habit of rolling your eyes."

Birty took a sharp intake of breath. "Look, sorry, I'm tired. I haven't had a lot of sleep, and Constable Smith called a few minutes ago to say he's going to be late in."

"You think you're the only one with problems? Out with it, I haven't got all day."

Birty rubbed his left eye. "After I left you yesterday, I got called back to the hospital. Daisy Rowbottom said a man and a woman pretending to be a doctor and nurse went around the hospital late yesterday procuring semen samples from patients."

Mayor Northan screwed up his face.

Birty stepped back and crossed his arms. "Apparently, they claimed all the men in the hospital had to be tested for a virus they called Bushranger's Revenge."

"And some of the patients agreed?"

"They *all* agreed."

"Oh, goodness me. Is Bushranger's Revenge even an ailment?"

"Daisy doesn't seem to think so."

"What would anyone want with semen?"

"Beats me. I don't even know if a crime has been committed and, if so, what crime? Is it *theft*? Or is it *obtaining substances under false pretences*? It might even be *rape*. I'll have to ask Stretch and Smithy. They seem to know all about these new-fangled crimes."

"How many men are in the hospital?"

"Fifteen, I think. I haven't interviewed all of the victims yet."

"Shouldn't you be interviewing the suspects first?"

"I haven't got any suspects yet."

Mayor Northan's eyes widened. "What about the bikers at The Applecart?"

"How could they be involved? They would have had to arrive 30 minutes before the newspaper said they pulled into town."

"The paper had a report on that too?"

Birty nodded.

"What about that bikie fellow we saw? He must surely be the other bikies' forward scout."

Birty leant forward, resting his elbows on the bench, locking his fingers and lowering his voice. "I don't mean to be rude, Mr Mayor. But this time you really need to leave the police work to the police."

Mayor Northan locked on to his eyes, determined not to blink first. "Do you really want me to report you to your superiors, sergeant? I'm sure they'll understand why I am annoyed you're trying to impede me from doing my civic duty to oversee the moral standards of this town."

Birty puffed out his cheeks and raised his palms. "Think about it for a minute. How could the bikie at the hospital possibly be involved?"

"It's quite plausible."

The sergeant snorted. "He told us he's lived in Blackstump Road for three years. He probably doesn't even know this new lot."

"Why not? He's a bikie isn't he?"

The sergeant raked his forehead. "As soon as I've got another pair of hands to help me, I'll check them out. OK?"

"What if they've already killed Whish-Willson and Rogerson by then?"

"*The Pick Of The Crop* says those blokes are in the pub of their own volition."

"I can't believe you're taking that rag's word over mine. *The Pick Of The Crop* has been getting its facts wrong since 1872. If Whish-Willson and Rogerson were free to leave, don't you think they would have come out by now?"

"That's not proof," Birty said. "Rog works in the pub and Wish-Wash takes a lot of budging when he's in a drinking mood."

"For goodness sake, sergeant, what more evidence do you want?"

"Screams . . . gun shots . . . a list of written demands from the bikers . . . anything really?"

Mayor Northan stamped his left foot again. "I don't think you're taking this seriously."

"Believe me, I don't want bikers in this town any more than you do. You heard me lay the law down to that Foetus fellow. But as far as I know this new lot haven't broken any laws."

"I saw them arrive, and some of them weren't wearing crash helmets. Isn't that against the law?"

"Of course it is, Jim."

The Mayor glowered. "What did you call me?"

"I meant to say *Mr Mayor*. Sorry. My point is this: How am I supposed to know which ones weren't wearing helmets?"

"They're in The Applecart right now."

"That doesn't prove anything. The law doesn't require motorcyclists to wear their helmets in the pub." Birty stretched his palms out in front of him and exhaled loudly. "But if it makes you feel better, I'll go and have a quiet talk to them now. You can come with me, too, if you like."

"No, er, um, I don't think I, er, um, need to on this occasion," Mayor Northan said. "It sounds like strictly police business to me."

––––––––

WHEN Johnno walked into the hospital room at 8.20am with the newspaper tucked under his arm, Foetus was propped up on his pillows with his arms crossed.

The bikie watched Johnno's frown deepen as he came closer to the bed.

"Haven't you seen someone wearing flannel pyjamas before?" Foetus unfolded his arms and waved his fist. "Before you ask, they're pictures of little Cherokee Indians. OK? Go on, laugh. I dare you, you little deviant."

Foetus hadn't slept well. Even though they had managed to bring his temperature down, he just couldn't stop thinking about those other bikers.

When a nurse came in to open the curtains at dawn, he quizzed her. "Do they call themselves The Thunderbirds?"

"Hmm." The nurse peered into the half light. "I can't be sure but the name does ring a bell."

As soon as the nurse left the room, Foetus stared at the window, wondering if it was about to blow, and bikie commandoes suddenly appear, comforting him with words along the lines, "No one gets left behind, bro". When something intruded on his thoughts, he looked up and saw Sister Rowbottom standing beside him.

She threw the PJs on the bed and told him to change out of the hospital gown "right now, mister". She said people had been complaining about his window display.

Johnno pinched the fabric at Foetus's shoulder. "I didn't even know they made those things in your size? Was yellow the only colour they had?"

"I wasn't given an option. The old cow said unless I agreed to swap my leather jacket, Big Bob wanted to have a go at his first enema. Does that sound like a threat to you?" He stared into the middle distance. "What kind of bloke even wants to do that to another bloke? He must be a poofter. Like you."

Johnno took in a sharp intake of breath and threw the paper on to the bed.

Foetus stared at it. "Does it have something about the gang across the road?"

"Yes, that's on Page Three, but you might want to look at the Back Page first. Moose got off. The umpire withdrew the report."

Foetus scooped the paper from the bed and turned to the back. He moved his lips as he scanned down the page, then looked up with puzzlement on his face. "This says the ump said he was actually 50 yards away!"

Johnno shook his head. "I don't know what's happened? But I know what I saw. The ump was right there."

Then he said, "I've got to go. I've got to report for my work orders."

Foetus put the paper down on his lap and crossed his arms again. "Moose and Lozza told me. But I reckon you got off lightly. I would have cut your dick off."

"Speaking of dicks, another article will probably interest you. It's on the Front Page."

———

DOBBER Leggs sent water flying when he slammed down his fist.

Reg Collins winced as he watched the resultant tsunami roll towards the edge of the spa and spill over.

Dobber Leggs held up a soggy copy of the newspaper with his other hand and yelled. "How many years have I tried to keep this kind of smut out of the pages? Who's responsible?" His voice echoed, and probably carried to the street.

Collins rubbed his chin. "The story has got your son's byline on it."

Dobber Leggs glared at the chief-of-staff and expelled the rest of his breath. "My son wouldn't have written this diatribe. Like this? Give him some credit, Reginald!"

It was 8.30am and Peter Salter had joined them for the morning news conference.

Salter, the municipal roundsman, had been invited so they might dissect the story he had been tasked to write for that day's Page One lead story. Only it wasn't there. The lead was about The Great Sperm Robbery.

Dobber Leggs stared at the wet Front Page, wishing the ink would smudge and disappear, and He'd wake up and realise this had been a bad dream.

He had been so happy, too, when he had left work at 6pm. Not only did he have in place a slick new night editor, he had left him with a cracker of a story to fill the Page One slot. It would breathe new life into an ongoing story of great interest.

The Mayor planned to take to council his plan to build Colonel Richard Northan's expensive bronze statue.

Salter had already talked to both James Northan and Deputy Mayor Peter Rowbottom.

Rowbottom, who was Daisy's bachelor brother, claimed the mayor's proposal would be an obscene waste of ratepayers' money. His opinion carried weight, too, because he controlled roughly half of the votes of the councillors.

The matter had been listed for discussion at the council meeting, after which the councillors would vote on it. This meant Salter couldn't finalise the story until after the vote. But no matter how the vote went, Dobber Leggs sensed the story would be a winner.

So it was with a spring in his step he went out to pick the newspaper off his lawn next morning.

When he unwrapped it and laid it down on the kitchen table, he could hardly believe his eyes.

If witnesses thought the splash he made in the spa moved the needle on the seismic scale, they should have heard the crash on the breakfast table. He had slammed his hand down so hard it sent crockery, cereal, milk and cutlery splashing and clanging over the tiled floor.

His temper didn't mellow after breakfast.

First, he put his bathers on backwards. Then he ignored the giveway sign at an intersection on the drive into the Dancing School. Normally he engaged in chit-chat with the woman on the front desk, but this morning he stormed right past her. If the Richter scale had measured human outbursts, he'd probably be up around 10.4.

"This is all Sean McWhirter's fault." The editor looked at Salter. "He didn't even run your story!"

"That's my fault, sir." Salter looked shamefaced. "I got the nights wrong. The council meeting is tonight."

"You what?" The editor felt the blood rising to his face.

"I got the night wrong, sir, I'm sorry."

Dobber Leggs stabbed at the air. "Not as sorry as McWhirter will be. I'll have his guts for garters for this. Reginald, I want you to get him on the phone and tell him I want to see him in my office A.S.A.P."

He climbed over the side of the spa like an angry hippopotamus, splashing even more water hither and thither. "I'm going back to the office to wait for him."

On the way to work, he ran into the Mayor walking from the police station. His face looked redder than Dobber Leggs's face felt.

"You! Bad enough this town is in the grip of a crime-wave, you've turned a respectable newspaper into a tabloid."

"Now hang on," Dobber Leggs said. "I'm not happy either. I'm going to sack the night editor as soon as I can."

"Your son Kevin wrote the damn article."

"The night editor obviously changed his copy."

"Is he Irish?"

"He's from Sydney. He's new. His name is Sean McWhirter."

"Who hired him, for goodness sake?" Mayor Northan asked.

"Reginald Collins did," the editor lied.

———

AFTER Johnno left his hospital room, Foetus re-read the Back Page story word for word. Then he flipped over the paper and read the story on the Front Page.

By Kevin Leggs

A BOGUS doctor and nurse yesterday escaped with a large amount of semen in a bizarre robbery at the Windy Mountain Hospital.

They enticed patients to provide sperm samples because they said they were checking for a viral infection called Bushranger's Revenge.

The chief investigating officer, Sergeant Randolph Birtwistle, said he was baffled by the crime.

"We don't know what we're dealing with yet. Until we do, I urge all citi-

zens to exercise extreme caution if approached by anyone fitting the descrip-
tions of the offenders."

The culprits escaped with their booty in a hospital beaker.

It is not known how many sperms this contained.

But given the average man releases 350 million sperm at a time, and at
least a dozen men were persuaded to contribute, the tally is believed to be well
into the billions.

The report was accompanied by identikit pictures of the bogus doctor
and nurse, which looked nothing like Moose and Lozza. This came as
no surprise to Foetus. He had mingled with plenty of criminals and he
hadn't seen a reliable identikit picture yet.

He turned the page and saw the story on the visiting bikers.

By Norman J. Hit

A GANG of bikers who arrived in Windy Mountain yesterday afternoon
have denied they are holding hostages in The Applecart hotel.

The Muttonbirds, a new Aboriginal gang from Hobart, say they are law-
abiding citizens who have been misunderstood.

Their leader, who goes by the single name of Foetus, said, "We're touring
the state on holidays and we thought this might be a good place to stop.

"We are enjoying the hospitality shown to us by barman Artie Rogerson
and one of your local characters, Wish-Wash."

Foetus said the bikers were open to offers of short-term employment.

"We're hard workers and we'll do just about anything," he said.

As Foetus scanned the page, he became conscious of a shadow cast on
his paper. Sister Rowbottom was standing behind him on the other
side of the bed, wasn't she? But when he turned his head, it wasn't her.
It was Bubby Throsby.

"Are they or aren't they?"

"Are they what?"

"Are they your gang?"

Foetus scowled.

"Another thing I don't understand is how come the Foetus in this story has the same name as you? Is it an Aboriginal name?"

"No, it is not." Foetus pointed to the skin on the back of his wrist. "Do I look Abo to you? *Really*? It's a bikie name. In bikie circles lots of people are called Foetus."

Bubby laughed. "You're pulling my leg."

Foetus looked at him blackly. "I hadn't thought of pulling your leg off."

With that, Bubby turned quickly. As he disappeared out the door, Foetus heard him say, "I just remembered . . ."

Normally Foetus might have roared with laughter. But he was in no mood for merriment. Foetus was hurting. Once again his hopes had been raised then shot down. On the rare occasions a bikie gang had passed through Windy Mountain it always turned out they were not The Thunderbirds. It wasn't even as if Foetus could get a transfer. Once a member of The Thunderbirds, always a member of The Thunderbirds even when they deserted you in rural Tasmania and stole your motorbike.

———

IF SEAN McWHIRTER even heard the phone ringing, he incorporated it into his dreams.

The call was coming from Tiger Kowalski's Dancing School where a dripping Reg Collins had commandeered the phone at reception.

It was 8.15am and McWhirter was in the deepest part of his sleep.

He had knocked off at 2am, and come home to an empty house with his mind still buzzing. What a debut shift it had been! First Dobber Leggs's Page One lead had fallen through, which had made him sick to his stomach. Then three corkers had fallen in his lap. He had no doubt which story deserved top billing but either of the others could have snagged the top spot on another day.

He stayed to check the first paper off the press, then went home a happy man.

McWhirter had landed on his feet in Windy Mountain.

He didn't really know how he had received such a glowing reference from his previous employers. His guess was they had just wanted to pass him along like a hot potato.

He had worked as a down-table subeditor in Sydney. He took his role as union representative much more seriously though and prided himself on being able to recite the award chapter and verse. What really irked his supervisors was he made sure his comrades knew all the ins and outs of industrial law too.

At 3am, he cooked himself a hearty fry-up meal, which he washed down with a glass of Guinness. Then he lowered himself into a bean bag and listened to Rory Gallagher CDs till the sun rose, which told him it was time to close the curtains and hit the sack.

"Where is he?" Collins said, as the phone rang and rang. Peter Salter was standing next to him, wrapped in a blue and white towel.

NINE
PAINTING THE TOWN GREEN

JOHNNO KNOCKED on the side of the open door.

An echoey voice inside the tin shed told him to come in.

Even though it sounded like the God of Thunder, Johnno knew the voice belonged to Oodles Noodle. He walked into the shadows and as his eyes adjusted to the light, he saw the works foreman sitting on a large toolbox. He was packing his pipe opposite two other blokes who were smoking cigarettes.

"We were just talking about you." Oodles sounded much less echoey in here. He pointed from one smoker to the other. "Meet my staff, Wacko, and that is Jacko. We're just having an early smoko."

Johnno stood in the middle of the shed and nodded to the two men. "Didn't you think I'd turn up?"

"It wasn't that. Jacko was wondering how come you didn't make today's newspaper? The whole town is talking about what you did."

"Maybe they had too much other stuff to go in?"

"Maybe so," Oodles started to laugh but it turned into a coughing fit. When he caught his breath, he said, "Not every day The Great Sperm Robbery takes place in this town."

"Or a bikie gang holes up at the pub?" Jacko said.

"Or Moose Routley gets off," Wacko said.

Oodles put a match to his pipe and sucked at the flame. When the pipe issued forth little smoke signals, he took it out of his mouth. "Yep, what happened there?"

Johnno rubbed the back of his neck. "I think Moose was as surprised as everyone else the umpire changed his mind."

Oodles rose, holding a hand on his back. "Follow me, Johnno, and I'll get you started."

They exited the shed and entered blinking into the daylight of the main yard past ride-on mowers, a rotary hoe, two tractors and a small grader. Apart from maintaining local roads, the council workers were also responsible for the upkeep of the Windy Mountain Recreation Area. The football oval needed constant watering, mowing and line-marking, especially with the grand final coming up. The netball court needed re-asphalting from time to time. The clay tennis court needed to be regularly swept and marked. The kiddies' play equipment needed frequent maintenance. Street and park trees needed to be lopped, the public toilets had to be kept in working order and one thing or another always needed painting.

Oodles stopped outside a small shed, and put his pipe on a post. "It wouldn't worry me if this whole lot went up in flames, but rules are rule. We can't smoke in here."

The shed was about the size of a one-car garage and it had a hefty padlock on the roller-door. Oodles dug his hand into his overalls pocket and produced a bundle of keys. He must have tried six of them before finding the one that fitted. Finally he was able to roll up the door to reveal a stack of hundreds of paint tins.

"This," Oodles said, "is one of the great investments of our austere men on the council . . . 300 gallons of green paint."

"What does the council want with 300 gallons of green paint?"

Oodles scratched his head. "It was Jim Northan's idea before the last State Budget. He told the council he had received inside informa-tion that paint was going to be hit with a big sales-tax hike. He persuaded them to buy all the green paint we could get our hands on."

"What happened?"

"We bought 300 gallons of the stuff." Oodles smiled wryly. "Between you and I, Jim Northan's brother-in-law supplied it all."

"But did the Mayor's inside information pan out?"

Oodles picked a strand of tobacco from his teeth, and flicked it to the ground. He grinned. "They hiked up the sales tax on petrol . . . grog went up . . . smokes went up . . . but green paint wasn't even touched."

"What are you going to do with it all?"

"Until they find a way to smoke paint or drink it, I guess we'll have to use it as plain old paint." Oodles shook his head. "The council won't let me buy any more until we've used up the paint we've already got."

Oodles selected a tin from the stack, picked up a stick that was lying on a bench, and prised off the lid. He stirred. "So slap on as much as you like."

Oodles was satisfied with the texture now. "Grab that brush over there," he said, pointing to a shelf, "and take this tin over to the football oval."

Johnno just stood outside the doorway, perplexed.

"I'm not carrying it for you, old son. I've got other work to do."

"But don't you want to supervise me?"

"You're not on a chain gang." Oodles smiled again. "But you won't get lonely. Another bloke is already over there." He pointed. "See."

Johnno glanced over to the footy ground where he saw an unmistakable figure kneeling at the boundary fence.

"The Big O is a regular so he'll show you what to do."

Johnno let out a big sigh. "I should have known I'd be seeing him again. How far around do you want me to paint?"

"Until you come to the end."

"But the boundary fence never ends; it keeps going around in a loop. How will I know when I come to the end?"

"How many hours of work orders did you get?"

"Eighty-two."

"That's how you'll know."

———

IT WAS true The Big O didn't sing. But he hadn't told Johnno he liked to whistle while he worked.

It wouldn't have been so bad if the noise he made had been tuneful.

But try bringing up the rear behind a tuneless whistler when the wind is blowing the strangled high-pitched soundbites of *it's a long way to Tipperary* your way!

Johnno tapped him on the back, and he turned. "Do you really have to make that racket?"

The Big O frowned. "No one has ever complained before."

"Maybe that's because you normally work here on your own?"

"Dat's a good point. Maybe we should swap positions? I'll try not to whistle but if I do, maybe you won't hear it."

This is what they were doing when a man walked across the oval towards them. He caught their eye because he was carrying a large stocking over his shoulder.

Only when he came closer did Johnno recognise him as Norman J. Hit, the newspaper reporter he had seen again only yesterday in court. He carried a notebook and had slung the stocking over his left shoulder.

He stopped when he reached them. "Is Oodles still trying to get rid of that green paint?"

The Big O rested his brush on the top of the tin at his feet. "Do you not want to write an exposé on it?"

Norman's shoulders slumped. "Everyone knows about the council stuff-up. But I don't think any report about it would get past my editor."

The Big O nodded from Norman to Johnno. "Do you two know each other?"

Johnno put down his paintbrush and said, "Yeah, we've met."

"Pity about your lawyer," Norman said.

Johnno rounded on The Big O and shook his index finger at him. "That reminds me, last time I take your advice!"

"Wasn't he any good?" The Big O said.

Norman J. Hit tutt-tutted. "Johnno would have been better off without him."

"I didn't exactly recommend him." The Big O straightened up. "You merely asked me if I *knew* any lawyers. Terry Mason always seemed like a toroughly decent fella to me. But if you had asked me what I tort about his legal skills, I would have given you a different answer."

Johnno kicked the ground.

"The ting is, dare's never any point in me engaging legal counsel. I'm always charged with drunk and disorderly conduct. I always plead guilty because I always *am* guilty. So why would I need a lawyer?"

After an awkward pause, Norman broke the silence. "Look on the bright side. We didn't put your name in the paper. My editor doesn't like smutty stories. He says ours is a *family* newspaper." He used his two index fingers to make quotation marks in the air.

The Big O voiced his surprise. "How does dat story you had on the Front Page today fit with your editor's morals?"

"Not well," Norman said. "Mr Leggs says it's the first time in the paper's 150-year history that *sperm*" — he drew quotation marks in the air again — "has appeared in *The Pick Of The Crop.*"

Johnno nodded towards the stocking slung over the reporter's shoulder. "isn't it a bit early to carry a Christmas stocking around?"

"Oh this?" Norman patted it. "No, this is a windsock. I'm doing research for an investigative feature piece on the wind. This windsock is so I can measure its velocity. But it's a good conversation piece too. I just met Mayor Northan in the High Street and he wanted to know all about it."

"Why would the Mayor be interested in wind socks?" The Big O said.

"He didn't say." Norman turned to leave. "Enjoy your painting."

THE arrival of The Muttonbirds in Windy Mountain was the best thing that had happened to Wish-Wash for at least 25 years. He captivated the bikers with his stories and, what's more, they believed almost every exaggerated word and never said anything about his orange trousers.

"Are you sure you're not Aboriginal?" asked the bikie with blue eyes and red hair.

"No, I was born in Sweden." *Hee-haw, hee-haw.*

"You tell a good story for a white fella," Bluey said.

He had that right. When it came to embellishing stories, no one was better in Windy Mountain. But Sweden? Any of the locals could have told you Bert Whish-Willson was a born and bred Windonian. It was only his dress-sense that seemed to come from somewhere else.

He had killed more than a few braincells over the past four decades. But his contemporaries reckoned he could have been the brightest student of his era had he knuckled down and spent less time playing football and fooling with girls. He had frequently topped classes in local and Australian history, without even trying, and he had read every science fiction book in the school library. He could have even have become a writer, so wild was his imagination and power of embellishment. But study was never a priority. He much preferred being the class clown.

Wish-Wash made a career decision at age 16. He dropped out of school, worked in some lowly paid jobs, started cultivating his fashion passions, and became town drunk when he was 19. By the time Wish-Wash claimed to have seen a Tasmanian Tiger in the High Street in his early 30s he was easily the best town drunk Windy Mountain had ever had.

But that alleged Thylacine sighting in 1967 changed things.

Many people had claimed to have seen the animal — mostly deep in the bush or on lonely country roads late at night. The observers had come from all walks of life: bushmen, rural taxi drivers, even the odd zoologist. But Wish-Wash was the first town drunk.

For the next two weeks he told anyone who would listen how he had been woken by a Tasmanian Tiger obviously inquisitive someone would be napping in the bus shelter in the High Street in the middle of the night. First it made it on to the front page of *The Pick Of The Crop*. A day or two later, the print and electronic media came from all over the world to interview him, usually in his familiar spot in the bar where he had a stool with his own nameplate, which the town had awarded him on Australia Day in recognition of his diligent service as town drunk for many years.

"Yeah," he drawled after taking yet another swig of his apple cider. "The Tasmanian Tiger is alive and kicking here in Windy Mountain." *Hee-haw, hee-haw.*

The locals did not believe a word of it.

Dobber Leggs was furious when he returned from holiday to find the moron he had left in charge of the newspaper had glorified the town drunk.

Mayor Northan was even angrier. Worried that Windy Mountain was becoming the laughing stock of the world, the Mayor took steps to make sure the story could never be verified. Then he started a campaign to destroy Wish-Wash's reputation.

It worked. Six weeks later the townsfolk replaced Wish-Wash as town drunk with the local Catholic priest. (the Big O was actually the third former priest to have a crack at the job)

Townsfolk now taunted Wish-Wash. "Here kitty, kitty, kitty," they would giggle.

"Hey, Wishy!" kids and grown-ups would often tease him. "Seen any Tasmanian Tigers lately?"

Wish-Wash found himself without not just a job but also without a public. At thirty-two, he was already too old to be re-trained into another job yet he was too young to be thrown on society's scrapheap. His self-esteem was shattered and he had spent his wilderness years trying to make ends meet by doing odd jobs.

The bikers gave him a whole new audience of admirers.

The cider kept coming and the bikers kept partying on all night. In the morning they bought a copy of *The Pick Of The Crop* to read about themselves, and they had a good laugh about the article on Page One about The Great Sperm Robbery.

"Why on earth would anyone want to nick semen?" Foetus wondered aloud.

"They're going to sell it to the Third World," Wish-Wash said, without even stopping to think most Third World countries already had more of the stuff than they could cope with.

The bikers savoured Wish-Wash's every word.

"Tell us more about that bikie in the hospital?" Foetus asked.

"He's got two broken legs and cirrhosis of the liver," Wish-Wash said. "And he wears leather pyjamas made from beasts he killed with his bare hands."

"Wow! What gang does he belong to?" Bluey asked.

Wish-Wash said the first thing that came into his head. "The Hells Angels."

Wish-Wash told them how The Applecart brewed its moonshine cider. "The apples are trampled by the town virgins; it's a Windy Mountain tradition."

He told them about Wee Jimmy McMartin's apple pies. "They're the best-tasting apple pies in Tasmania. The apples are nurtured at night by a local ghost."

And he told them about the night he saw the Tasmanian Tiger.

"I thought the Tasmanian Tiger was extinct?" said the bikie they called Frizzle, probably because of his massive frizzy beard that made him look like a prototype for ZZ Top.

"I've seen one with my own eyes here in the High Street."

"Wow!" one of the women said

"I saw him quite clearly. I was taking a nap in the bus shelter on the way home from the pub, and he woke me up. He was so close to me I was able to pat him."

"Wow!" came the chorus.

"As I told all the newspapers," he continued after taking another swig of his cider," he stood in front of me for a good two minutes before scampering off up the street."

Foetus tugged at his beard. "I heard some Japanese billionaire had offered a $100,000 reward for anyone who could prove the Tasmanian Tiger wasn't extinct?"

Wish-Wash shook his head. "Trouble is, I can't prove it."

"What did he look like?"

"He had a dog's face. He had stripes on his back, a tail like a kangaroo's and jaws that opened full stretch like a crocodile's."

Bluey's eyes widened. "How close did you say you were to him?"

"Close enough to smell his breath."

"Really!" Frizzle said. "What did that smell like?"

Wish-Wash said the first thing that came into his head.

"Apples."

TEN

QUICK! CALL IN THE ARMY

BIRTY INTERVIEWED everyone of interest at the Windy Mountain Hospital and came to the conclusion Mayor Northan and himself were chief suspects in The Great Sperm Robbery.

The receptionist had as much as said so with her accusing look. "Everyone saw you and the Mayor here at the hospital yesterday."

"But surely you saw someone else?" Birty said.

She shook her head. She had been so distracted by the sight of the two officials in all their finery, Moose and Lozza hadn't even registered in her memory banks.

Birty interviewed the bikie with suspected hepatitis and the sprained ankle, but to no avail.

"The first I knew about it was when I read the newspaper this morning," Foetus said. "It wasn't you and the Mayor, was it? You were in the hospital around that time."

Bubby said he didn't know anything either. He had been in the bath.

Birty interviewed 13 patients who admitted they had contributed but none of them could or would add to the evidence, except to say the doctor appeared to know what he was talking about and the nurse seemed to know what she was doing.

Henry Henderson, a patient with Alzheimer's Disease, claimed to have been a victim, too, but Sister Rowbottom doubted it. "He's 88 and I don't think his evidence would stand up in court or anywhere else."

Birty interviewed the doctor who had been on roster at the time of the robbery and three nurses. He talked to a cleaner and a hospital cook. But nobody had noticed anything . . . except his and Mayor Northan's presence at the hospital near the time of the crime.

———

MAYOR Northan thumped the desk of council-clerk Hilda Hinchcliffe. "Why can't I proclaim martial law?"

"You're not authorised to do that." Mrs Hinchcliffe rose from her chair to bring her large frame up to the same level as the Mayor who stood on the other side of her desk. She could see Mayor Northan was really worked up, even more worked up than he usually got. His face was beetroot red. He was waving a fist in the air.

"Local government heads aren't allowed to declare martial law," Mrs Hinchcliffe said.

"Well, who is?"

"I don't know. The Premier perhaps?"

"Get him on the phone then."

"And tell him what exactly?"

"Tell him about the crime-wave happening in Windy Mountain."

"What crime-wave?"

"For goodness sake, woman, haven't you read *The Pick Of The Crop* today?" Mayor Northan said.

"Of course I have."

"Didn't you read about the bikers who stole the semen from the hospital?"

"It didn't say that! The bikers and the robbery were featured in two separate articles if I remember correctly."

Mayor Northan snarled. "Read between the lines, you stupid fat woman."

Mrs Hinchcliffe's voice went up an octave. "You can't talk to me like that!"

"Why not? I'm the Mayor."

"I couldn't care less who you are. You mind your mouth."

Hilda Hinchcliffe was indeed a big woman. In fact, she was the largest, most imposing woman in Windy Mountain and the floral dress with the big patterns she wore today made her look even larger and even more imposing. But she wasn't stupid. She had been the council clerk for 22 years, and she had become used to the tantrums of Mayor Northan, who had been in that job even longer. He bullied her and he insulted her. But this was the first time he had got worked up enough to ask that martial law be declared in Windy Mountain.

"Look," Mayor Northan said. "You don't seem to realise Windy Mountain has been invaded by hoodlums. It's the biggest threat to the safety of this town since the Irish first came here."

"Aren't you over-reacting? The report in the newspaper said the bikers in The Applecart are hard-working tourists."

"Hardworking? What work do you think they've ever done? They're probably hitmen and hired baby-killers."

"Come off it." Mrs Hinchcliffe picked up a copy of the newspaper from the top of a filing cabinet, turned to Page Three and pointed at the report on The Muttonbirds. "They're high-spirited young lads. It says here, see, they like our town and would like to get some local work."

"Over my dead body!" Mayor Northan said. "They'll never work in this town; I'll see to that."

"How are you going to stop them?"

"I'll have them evicted by the army."

"Windy Mountain hasn't got an army. All we've got is a grumpy old police sergeant and two constables."

"I'm talking about the Australian Army," Mayor Northan said. "When martial law is declared, the army always takes over."

"I hate to break this to you, but your jurisdiction as mayor starts with sewage and ends with stormwater."

Mayor Northan stamped his foot. "Never mind telling me things I'm *not* allowed to do. Tell me what I *am* allowed to do."

"In this case, I advise you to do nothing. If you insist on ringing the Premier, Windy Mountain Council will become a laughing stock."

"And what about the crime-wave?"

"It will just be a memory this time next week. I wouldn't worry about it if I were you."

"Wouldn't worry?" Mayor Northan's voice reached a new level of shrillness and the veins in his neck looked ready to burst. "You don't know what these bikie hoons are capable of? While they are in this town, no one is safe out on those streets. Even you. They're not fussy."

She glared at him.

He held his hands in front of him, which was the nearest he ever came to apologising, and spoke in a calmer voice. "If you won't call the Premier, will you at least call an emergency council meeting?"

"Have you forgotten we already have a meeting scheduled for 8 o'clock tonight," Mrs Hinchcliffe said. "How could you forget your proposal for the statue? I faxed the agenda to everyone this morning?"

"Can't we bring the meeting forward to 6 o'clock. It's urgent we discuss what to do. And besides, I have another thing I need to be discussed too."

"Another thing? Two things to spring on council without warning?" Mrs Hinchcliffe sighed.

———

AFTERNOON SHADOWS were creeping over the football oval as The Big O and Johnno continued to inch their way around the boundary.

The Big O stepped back to admire his handiwork. "What do the footballers think about having a green boundary fence?"

"How would I know?"

"Hasn't Moose Routley ever mentioned it?"

Johnno stopped his brushwork and gazed into the middle distance. "Now you mention it, a few weeks ago he asked me if I liked the colour. I thought it was an odd thing to ask me because being from Queensland I didn't even know the footy rails ought to be white, not green. But he said that was the colour our house was going to be painted, which made no sense at the time. Now it does."

"Why didn't Moose go to the fancy dress party wit' you?"

"He said he was going to, but I should have known he'd jump at any excuse to pull out." Johnno pouted as he started painting again. "I just wish I had stuck to the original plan to go as one of the caped crusaders. Didn't seem to make much sense when Batman got reported though."

The Big O resumed his painting. As far as he was aware, he had resisted all urges to whistle. Certainly, Johnno hadn't complained again. What followed was five minutes where the sole sound was the swishing and slapping of brushes.

Johnno broke the silence. "Do you believe in the existence of the Tasmanian Tiger?"

"I wouldn't like to say."

"Why not?"

"The Tasmanian Tiger got poor ol' Wish-Wash into a lot of hot water."

"Yeah, but no one believed him," Johnno said. "It's different with you. Priests don't tell lies."

"Well, I've never seen a Tasmanian Tiger."

"So you don't believe in it?"

"I didn't say dat. I've never seen God either but dat doesn't mean I don't believe."

After five more minutes of the sound of brushwork and paint drying, The Big O asked, "Are you going to the grand final?"

"Of course." Johnno laughed. "I plan to be there with belles on. Don't tell Sergeant Birtwistle."

The Big O starred at him blankly. "Oh, I might see you at the ground den. Or you might see me."

He wasn't trying to be cryptic. He was usually the first person at the ground on game day, which was one of the perks of sleeping in one of the coach's boxes. Even though this was the grand final, he doubted he'd vary from his routine. How it normally went was he'd spend most of the early game time in the bar and only go outside at quarter-time for a pie when the crowds came in. He usually left the bar again just before halftime because he was usually half cut by then and the bar staff were happy to lend a shoulder before the next rush. The Big O would be happy to leave. By then, he was usually looking for a good place to lie down.

———

IF THE greenies hadn't called it quits for the day they would never have seen Mayor Northan sitting on the bench opposite the police station. He was reading *The Financial Review*.

The quartet had spent all day around the farmhouse table trying to decide how best to save the Tasmanian Tiger.

"The trouble is," William had said, "if the Tasmanian Tiger really does still exist, we haven't got a clue where it hangs out."

"Wish-Wash saw it in the High Street, man," John said.

"I've said it before, Wish-Wash tells lies," William said. "Why can't we revert to our previous course of action of saving the Green Swift Parrot?"

"Because we *voted* against it," Dilly said.

"But it was a silly vote."

This argument went around in circles for hours until Sarah moved a motion they have a time out. "We can go into town, buy a newspaper, get some apple pies from the bakery and resume our discussion in the morning."

They saw the Mayor as they passed by on the other side of the High Street on their way to Wee Jimmy McMartin's bakery.

If Mayor Northan noticed them, he didn't show it.

He didn't even flinch when Sergeant Birtwistle stopped right in front of him, on his way back from the hospital.

"Mr Mayor, this is the last place I'd expect to find you."

"It's the first time I've stopped all day, sergeant." Mayor Northan lowered his newspaper. "I found another good article about the wind-sock industry. Want to see it? Apparently, it's all the rage in Scandinavia. Those Vikings turned pillage into a fine art for accumulating wealth, so you have to think they know what they are doing. My offer still stands if you want to join me."

"I thought you were more concerned about the so-called *crime-wave*?"

"I most certainly am," Mayor Northan said. "That's why I've pushed that issue up to second on the council meeting agenda tonight."

"Have you really thought this through? I predict there will be a public outcry if you manage to even get permission."

"Of course I'll get permission," Mayor Northan snorted. "I'm the Mayor."

"Maybe," the sergeant said. "But name me one man in Windy Mountain who is going to help you remove that orchard?"

"Money talks," Mayor Northan said. "I'm sure I will have workers queuing up once I pass the word."

"We'll see."

"Mark my words, you'll be sorry you didn't come aboard." He let that sink in, then said, "What did you find out at the hospital, sergeant?"

"Nothing, really."

"Are the bikers in The Applecart among your suspects?"

"Yes, but only after you and me."

"What did you say?"

"Nothing."

"I thought you said you were going to see them?"

"I did. Didn't you get my message?"

"Why haven't you moved them on then? You must know riff-raff like that are very bad for the business health of this town."

"How do you figure that?"

The Mayor looked pained. "Do you really think they are paying for their drinks? Yet while they are there, no actual paying customers can get into The Applecart."

"Swings and roundabouts, Mr Mayor. Beryl over at the Wind Tunnel Cafe reckons they've never been busier."

Birty and Mayor Northan were too involved in their discussion to notice the greenies return from the bakery with their apple pies. Nor did they see them come out of the general store with a few groceries and a copy of *The Pick Of The Crop*. They didn't even notice them standing outside the shop huddled over their newspaper and having a good giggle over the report on The Great Sperm Robbery.

ELEVEN
TIGER'S TALE

IF PEOPLE HAD KNOWN something of Tiger Kowalski's background, it would have helped explain why he behaved the way he did.

Tiger's earliest memory had nothing to do with a football at all.

His earliest memory was of lying next to his father in a cavity secreted beneath a car boot. He was nearly four years old and he had been told it was a game of hide-and-seek.

He had no idea how long he was in the hidey hole, he just remembered it was a tight squeeze, it was dark and he had to pee in one bottle and drink from another. He also remembered his father cupping his little mouth every time the car came to a halt and they heard the strange voices and the boot open above them.

He'd never forget being finally discovered.

This time, the boot being opened wasn't the only noise.

The false bottom that secreted them was also peeled away, drenching their hiding place in almost unbearable light. A man in a uniform looked down at them smiling and said something in a language he couldn't understand.

As he grew up, he learned the language the man spoke was German. And what he had said was, "Welcome to West Germany."

He also learned he and his father had got through many border crossings to flee from their homeland. If they had been caught, his dissident father probably would have been shot. And Tiger, whose actual name was Tigran, wouldn't be standing here on a Tuesday afternoon in September watching his players arrive for training ahead of the grand final.

Tigran's mother and father were dead now but they would have been proud of what he had made of himself, and felt vindicated they had settled in this country. His mother and sister managed to flee their homeland 11 months after his father and him. When he was nearly six they moved to Australia, and his father found work on the Snowy Mountain Scheme. Later they moved to the west coast of Tasmania where his father laboured on the hydro-electricity scheme. By his early teens, Tigran was playing the tough brand of Aussie Rules they played on the west coast. Soccer, his father's first choice of sport, was regarded as a game for sissies.

Tiger skirted around the minor leagues in Tasmania for years. When he was available, he went where the money was. When he wasn't available, he was doing a bit of jail time, mainly for grievous bodily harm. He never started the fights but he always finished them. He was recruited by Windy Mountain in the twilight of this stop-start career. By then, he was 35 and had lost a yard or two of pace, but niggling injuries didn't end his career. Rather it was the realisation he was a marked man in the eyes of umpires that caused him to retire. Was it his fault so many opposition players keeled over from sunstroke in his vicinity?

He was asked to stay on as coach. But that job didn't pay more than beer money, so he came up with a counter-proposal. How about the club set him up in his own business? Tiger Kowalski's Dancing School was born.

And now Windy Mountain was on the cusp of winning its first premiership in nearly a century of trying. The club had been one of the foundation members of the league in 1894 but hadn't cracked it yet.

Tiger stood on a bench next to the doorway and clapped as the players entered. He had got his volunteers to decorate the inside of the shed in black and yellow bunting. He wanted to whip the players into a state of excitement, to make them realise they could make history.

First in was Wee Jimmy McMartin, who had a thick Scottish accent only the Chinese greengrocer, Hoo-Chung Loo, understood.

Close behind him were Loo, butcher Manny Hjorth, who was nicknamed the Flying Dutchman even though he was from Belgium and rarely got off the ground, and the ever-hopeful Billy Gumboots.

Others soon arrived, and the shed became grand final central station. Trainers strapped players and rubbed them down. Spiros Firos, an expatriate Greek who ran a souvlaki shop in Launceston and played in the key centre half-forward position, sat on a bench and sucked at a cigarette. It made the shed hazy, and the smell of smoke mingled with the smell of liniment.

By the time Moose arrived, last as usual, the other players were ready to run out.

Instead, they stood either side of the door and made a path for him to walk through, like Moses crossing the Red Sea. They didn't know how he had beaten the charge. They didn't care. All they knew was he was the player who could lead them to the promised premiership.

"Nice of you to join us," Tiger said, as he came through the door.

Moose looked up, and saw the coach dressed in his leather jacket. "I couldn't find my boots."

"You mean my boots," Billy Gumboots said.

It wasn't the first time Tiger had glared at young Billy. If only he knew how much it had cost him to ensure Moose would be allowed to play in the grand final! Umpires who dropped reports didn't come cheap. It had cost Tiger $2000 and a gold membership to the Dancing School. All Billy had had to give up was a pair of lousy football boots and a regular place in the team.

Tiger thanked the day could hardly believe his luck the day Moose had turned up looking for a game.

He was the type of player Tiger knew he needed. Heck, he looked as if he were cut from the same stone as Tiger. Brain and brawn.

The bloke got better with every game.

The only shocker he played all year was in the second semifinal against Slutz Plains, and that wasn't his fault.

Windy Mountain didn't have to win that game because it had finished on top of the ladder, thus earning a double chance.

And once Tiger got his bet on, he was quite happy to engineer a surprise loss. First he tinkered with the team at the selection table. Several key players got the chop, which gave him the excuse to play other players in odd positions in an attempt to fill the holes. His No. 1 rover spent the game at full-forward, for instance, and Wee Jimmy, all 5 foot 4 of him, contested the rucking duels.

He didn't drop Moose — for fear it would be seen as too obvious he was throwing the game.

But he wasn't silly. He made sure the water bottles the runners took out to Moose were spiked with sedatives. He was amazed the big man didn't curl up on the ground and go to sleep. He didn't, but the ploy still worked.

The Saints won easily and Tiger became $2000 richer — only to lose all of it bribing the umpire a bit more than a week later.

He watched the players run out, and followed them to the gate.

They set off for their first warm-up lap of the oval, which looked a picture even in the fading light. Three sprinklers had been placed strategically on the driest points of the ground. The rest of the oval had a good covering of grass which was almost as green as the freshly painted rails around the oval. Moose didn't appear from the sheds until the players had nearly completed their second lap and he joined the front of the pack, which didn't go down well with the jeering players at the back.

Billy led the runners, which was surprising because his gumboots had always slowed him down, yet now he was hellbent on impressing the selectors. He even managed to turn his head and gasp to the others, "Did you hear about the bikers? First, they robbed the hospital. Now they're holding Wish-Wash and Rog hostage in the pub."

"How do you know they're being held hostage?" Moose was happy for the rumour mill to deflect attention away from him.

"I saw Birty go into the pub," puffing Billy said. "I think he's trying to negotiate with them."

"I bet there wasn't much money to steal from the hospital?" Moose said.

"Who said anything about money? They got away with a beaker full of semen," Billy said.

"Semen! What would bikers want with semen?" Moose stepped up his running and surged ahead.

———

MOOSE had barely come through the door when Lozza thrust a copy of *The Pick Of The Crop* at him.

He tried waving it away. "We've got work to do. I haven't got time to read this."

"But you have to look. They've run our photos."

Moose's eyes widened as he sat down and examined the paper. Soon he began to laugh. He held up the page that had the identikit photos. "These could be anyone! Have you ever seen the Bonnie and Clyde movie?"

Moose's hair was still slicked back from his shower after training, so he guessed he did look like a gangster.

Moose's guess was some of the patients who had given the police artist their bogus recollections would have known fine well who he was. As for Lozza, he guessed none of them were about to confess to their wives they had succumbed to the soothing left hand of a hostess at the Dancing School, who was off on sick leave.

Moose put the paper down. "Relax, no one is going to blab. You'll get some money out of this."

He rolled up his sleeves as he got up and walked to the other end of the kitchen table, which he had set up earlier. The beaker of stolen goods was surrounded by dozens of little test tubes and a bunch of tags, some of them with names written on in blue ink.

Lozza watched as he started funnelling the stolen semen into the test tubes, which he then corked and attached a tag to.

"Give me some more bushrangers' names."

Lozza smiled thinly. "Ned Kelly?"

"I've already flooded the market with Ned's whiskers."

"OK then. What about Mad Dog Morgan?"

Moose stopped his funnelling and stared at the wall. "Why didn't I think of Mad Dog? The Americans would love a name like that."

Lozza spotted one tag she wasn't comfortable with. "Errol Flynn wasn't a bushranger."

"He *was* a Tasmanian."

"But he definitely wasn't a bushranger."

Moose laughed. "If anyone asks, I'll tell them Errol Flynn was a bushranger in Tasmania before he went to Hollywood to become a pirate and Robin Hood."

Lozza continued to watch Moose work. "Do you think that billionaire friend of yours will really be able to market this stuff?"

"Are you kidding? They'll probably cut it with something to make it go further, but I expect every drop will be packaged in little capsules as part of jewellery and good luck charms, and billed as genuine Australian bushrangers' by-products."

———

MAYOR Northan looked at his watch. "It's on the stroke of eight o'clock so let's cut the chit-chat and get this meeting started."

He glared down at the back of Hilda Hinchcliffe. "You have the council clerk to thank for not being home by now. She wouldn't let me bring the start time forward."

Everyone on the Windy Mountain council had arrived in high spirits. It was grand final week, after all, and the local team was the talk of the town. But exactly what Mrs Hinchcliffe predicted happened as soon as she handed out the agenda around the big oblong table. When she resumed her seat, she watched the faces of the councillors contort as they read what the new first item of business was.

Mrs Hinchcliffe had warned him. It was bad enough he insisted on sitting alone up there in the magistrate's elevated position, thinking he was some kind of superior being. But this wasn't the kind of project he could ram through the council. Even the Mayor had to fill out the official forms and submit them to relevant council officers, and get planning approval in principle before could be discussed by council.

To her left, the chair of Councillor Peter Rowbottom squealed as he stood and waved the new agenda. "You have a hide!" He glared up at the Mayor. "When I came here tonight I was ready to oppose the ridiculous waste of public money paying homage to your oppressive relative." He turned and looked at the faces of his supporters around the table. "I wasn't alone either."

This brought on a chorus of grunts that sounded to Mrs Hinchcliffe like support. This is what she had told the Mayor would happen. She had warned him Councillor Rowbottom had been rallying the troops behind the scenes. But he had dismissed him as a threat because he said he was limp-wristed, an accusation Mrs Hinchliffe had warned him never to repeat in public. "Don't dare call him Bumface either. You're not back in the schoolyard."

Councillor Rowbottom waved the agenda again. "This shows your arrogance has no bounds. No moral compass, whatsoever! You really want permission to destroy that orchard to build, of all things, a windsock factory? It's preposterous!"

These comments started the landslide that followed.

Councillor Michael McMichael accused Mayor Northan of vandalism.

"I'm not voting for it," Councillor Arthur Thomson said.

"Neither am I," Councillor Spot Billings said. "The ghost of Colonel Richard Northan will be very angry indeed."

"My granddaughter was weaned on those apples," Councillor Steve Morton said.

"One of my ancestors was the orchard's first foreman," Councillor George Railings said.

Mayor Northan reached for his gavel and brought it down with a thud. "Now listen to me," he barked. "As the Mayor, I think I am in an excellent position to know what's best for this town."

"You shouldn't even be involved in this discussion," Councillor Stefan Panitzki said. "It's not right; you've got a pecuniary interest."

"Yes, why don't you leave the room?" Councillor Jeff Deeth said.

"I'll do nothing of the sort. I have been elected by the citizens of Windy Mountain to represent them and give leadership to this motley council. That's what I intend to do."

"What about Jimmy McMartin's apple pies?" Councillor Dutchy Van Der Haag asked. "Jimmy gets his apples from the Northan orchard."

"That's right!" Councillor Harold Hawthorn-Jones said. "And where do you think they get the ingredients for the apple cider they sell at The Applecart?"

Mayor Northan screamed down at them. "Where I sell my apples is none of this council's business."

"It's relevant to your application," Councillor Morton said.

"Look," the Mayor said. "I thought I was doing the right thing seeking council approval. But I warn you: I will proceed with my plans with or without your consent."

"You can't do that!" Councillor Rowbottom said.

"I think you'll find I can."

"It's unlawful," Councillor Billings said.

"I'm the Mayor. In this town, I am the law."

"No one in this town will help you," Councillor McMichael warned. "That orchard might be in your name but it belongs to us all. It's our heritage."

"No one's going to tell me what or what not to do with my own land," the Mayor shouted. "I thought you people would have known better. It's progress I am interested in, not heritage. I don't care if I have to bring workmen in from the mainland."

Councillor McMichael was the first to leave. He waved a finger at Mayor Northan as he backed towards the exit. "You've gone too far this time. I'm not going to be a party to this. It's corruption." He slammed the door behind him.

Councillor Rowbottom followed, then a bunch of others left.

At this point Mayor Northan threatened to sack the next person to leave.

Councillor Morton responded by trying to move a no confidence motion in Mayor Northan.

"You can't do that," the Mayor snapped. "We no longer have a quorum."

"Is that right? I'm going home then." Councillor Morton got up and headed for the door.

"So am I," Councillor Panitzki followed.

Four remaining councillors looked at each other, then got up and left too.

"But we haven't discussed what to do with the bikers yet?" shouted Mayor Northan to their backs.

It was 8.15pm

"What did I do?" The Mayor directed this to Mrs Hinchcliffe and not Peter Salter, who had been sitting quietly in the press box at the side of the room recording the meeting in shorthand. "I didn't even get the chance to raise the matter of the statue, let alone ask what we're going to do about the bikers holed up in The Applecart?"

Salter raised his hand. "Excuse me, Mayor Northan."

The Mayor jumped. "What are you doing here?"

"Does this mean the meeting is over?"

Mayor Northan snorted. "isn't that what it looks like?"

"I must have received the wrong agenda." Salter looked puzzled as he held up a wad of stapled green sheets of paper. "None of the topics on my list have been discussed. What am I going to put in the paper tomorrow?"

Mayor Northan cleared his throat as a look of panic came on his face. "You certainly can't print anything said tonight."

"Why not?"

"Because . . . because . . . because it was all in camera. I thought you would have guessed that? Don't forget I know your editor well."

TWELVE
WRATH OF THE MAYOR

"NOT AGAIN?" Dobber Leggs grimaced as soon as he saw the headline on the front page. It was 6.30am and he was in his dressing gown and pyjamas on his front lawn. He nearly tripped over the family cat, Mr Bojangles, as he walked back towards the front door reading the report as he went.

COUNCIL UPROAR!
Mass walkout as Mayor threatens
to pull out historic apple orchard

It only got worse.

By Peter Salter
THE Windy Mountain council meeting was thrown into turmoil last night when 11 councillors walked out in protest at plans by Mayor James Northan to remove his historic family orchard.

Mayor Northan unexpectedly sought council approval to rip out the orchard and build a windsock factory on the site.

Fifteen minutes after the start of the meeting, the other councillors stormed out after accusing the Mayor of trying to bulldoze his project through council.

Mayor Northan, however, was defiant. "No one is going to tell me what to do with my own land. I don't care if I have to bring workmen in from the mainland."

Mayor Northan later tried to gag this newspaper from reporting the events of the meeting. He left the chambers in a huff.

When Dobber Leggs opened the screen door, he heard the phone ringing inside. By the time he got to the end of the hallway his wife Ruby had answered it.

"It's for you," she whispered. "Mayor Northan sounds furious."

He took the phone, held it to his chest and tried to think what he was going to say. With any luck, the Mayor hadn't even seen the newspaper yet and he was still angry about yesterday's edition.

Dobber Leggs summoned the courage to talk cheerfully into the mouthpiece.

"Good morning, Mr Mayor."

"Don't *good morning* me."

The Mayor was screeching so loudly, he had to hold the receiver well away from his ear. But he could still hear him loud and clear. "You and your newspaper have gone too far this time. I want the head of that reporter on a stick, you hear? That whole meeting was in camera, and I made this very clear to him. Don't be surprised if you are expelled from the Masonic Lodge, where I have a lot of influence. Expect to hear from the Press Council too."

Dobber Leggs re-engaged the phone. "You know, hardly anyone reads our very insignificant newspaper any more. I'd be surprised if the Press Council even knows we exist."

"Don't think I don't know what you are trying to do? Lots of people are reading your grubby little rag after yesterday's debacle —

including me. And just as well I am, too, otherwise I wouldn't have seen the new levels you have sunk to."

"I had nothing to do with today's front page."

"You're the editor, for goodness sake! If you're not responsible for this, who is?"

"Sean McWhirter."

"I thought you said you were going to sack him?"

"I told Reginald Collins to."

"Did he or didn't he?"

"Hard to tell. I had to leave the office early yesterday before McWhirter started work." That was Ruby's fault. He had to admit he was the one who had had the sudden spike in high blood pressure. But she was the one who had insisted he get an appointment with his doctor as soon as he could, even if he had to leave the office earlier than usual. "Judging by the front page, he's still running things though. What can I say? I'm so, so angry myself. So, so sorry."

By the time the editor had finished getting them out, he realised the phone was now beeping at him because the Mayor had hung up.

Ruby called out from the kitchen. "I could hear him shouting from here. What did he want this time?"

"Nothing to worry about, dear." By then, the editor was at his desk in the study flicking through his address book for Collins's number.

———

THE BIG O gave his position away. His snoring echoed around the Windy Mountain Football Ground.

Johnno wheeled his bicycle around the road that circled the oval. As he approached the home coach's box, the noise became louder — each snort ending with a little whistle.

He quietly leant his bicycle against the fence, ducked under the rail, tip-toed to the front of the box and took a peek at the sleeping figure. The Big O was covered in a tattered blanket, his head rested on a faded blue sports bag.

He awoke with a startle. "What? Who's dat?" He brought a hand up to his face to use as a sunshield.

"It's me."

"Johnno? Why are you whispering?"

"I didn't want to wake anyone."

"Bit late for dat." The Big O sat up, looked around and scratched his head. Then he saw how low the sun was in the sky. "What time is it?"

Johnno looked at his watch. "Five to seven."

The Big O rubbed his eyes. "Jesus, Mary, and Joseph. What do you tink you are you doing here at dis hour?"

Johnno pinched the bridge of his nose. "I couldn't sleep. I tossed and turned all night worrying how Moose got off that striking charge. I saw him hit that guy, and Moose even told me why he had done it. Now the umpire tells the tribunal he was a long way away and couldn't see it at all. Something's not right."

"Perhaps you should just be glad he's free to play in the grand final?"

Johnno blew air from his cheeks. "You're right. You go back to sleep. I'll start work."

"No, I'm awake now." The Big O threw off his blanket and swung his feet to the ground.

He folded up his blanket neatly and tucked it inside the sports bag he had been using as a pillow. "Give me ten minutes."

He headed out across the ground towards the toilet and shower block on the other side of the oval.

———

"WHY HAVEN'T you fired Sean McWhirter?" Dobber Leggs shouted.

"I tried," Reg Collins said. "But he says he hasn't done anything wrong."

The editor picked up the newspaper and hurled it across the black-wood desk in his office. "Have you seen today's front page?"

"Of course I have. *Before* you called me this morning too. I tried ringing McWhirter, too, but he didn't answer so I rang Peter Salter to get his side of the story. He wasn't happy about being dragged out of bed to answer the phone. But he says the report is fair and accurate."

"Do you know what time the Mayor rang me at home this morning?"

"Let me guess? Right before you rang me?"

"I don't think you realise the gravity of the situation you're in, Reginald."

"The situation *I'm* in?"

"If you had done what I asked, you would have fired McWhirter yesterday."

"But I told you, he wouldn't let me sack him."

The editor peered over the top of his glasses, which were almost on the tip of his nose. "isn't that for us to decide?"

"Not according to him. He quoted union rules, chapter and verse too. These days you can't sack someone unless you have a very, very watertight reason."

The editor's voice rose again. "We have *two* very, very watertight reasons: *yesterday's* newspaper and *today's* newspaper. We've already had sperm robberies and municipal mayhem. What's coming next, for goodness sake?"

"All I know is yesterday's newspaper looked good and we sold more copies than usual."

"I hated it. Sergeant Birtwistle really hated it and Mayor Northan really, really hated it."

"But McWhirter doesn't care about that. He reckons he was just doing his job."

"What's his excuse for today's paper?"

"How do I know? I told you, he didn't answer his phone."

"Can't we sack him for that?"

"Fair go." Collins looked at the clock on the wall. "It's not even 8am and he's probably still asleep. Haven't you ever done a night shift?"

"Why can't you send a car to haul him in here?"

"The office hasn't got his address."

"For crying out loud, Reginald. You didn't have his address yesterday morning. Why didn't you get it when he came to work?"

"I didn't think I'd need it again."

"Why not?"

"Because you told me to sack him."

"But you didn't sack him."

"How was I to know he would throw me off guard with his knowledge of union regulations?"

The editor looked upwards as if he were seeking divine guidance. "Do I have to do everything around here myself?"

"Everything?" Reg Collins said. "When was the last time you fired *anyone*?"

"I've fired lots of people."

"Name one?"

The editor leant back in his chair and thought for a moment. "That Bob Higgins fellow from Melbourne."

"You *hired* Bob Higgins. I was the one who had to *fire* him."

Dobber Leggs thought for a moment more. "That dreadful reporter Scott Smithies. I fired him."

"No, you didn't. You hired him, remember? You said he was Walkley Award material."

Dobber Leggs looked at the floor. "Well, yes. But that's one of the rare times I've been wrong. I think I coughed up to that at the time."

"But you didn't fire him. You told *me* to do that."

"The trouble with you is you haven't yet learned to take a share of responsibility."

"You've never fired anyone, have you?"

"I'm a busy man. Sometimes I have to delegate." The editor shook his head from side to side. "Stop trying to change the subject anyway. What exactly did Peter Salter tell you about today's report?"

"He said he didn't really want to write it that way. McWhirter told him to. But he also said what went in the paper was a fair record of what went on."

"And you believed him?"

"I've never had reason to question his accuracy. He takes the best shorthand in the office."

"Mayor Northan says he's going to take this further."

"If he really plans to destroy that orchard what this newspaper says about it will be the least of his worries."

"Mayor Northan said we had no right to report the council meeting because it was held in camera."

"Salter is adamant it wasn't. He says Mayor Northan only tried to tell him it was after the meeting."

"And you believed him!"

"Peter has been covering council meetings for years. He knows the difference between open and closed meetings."

"I still want you to sack McWhirter."

At that moment came a knock at the door. Dobber Leggs looked up at the clock. "Yes, come in," he barked.

———

"AM I interrupting something?" Norman J. Hit surveyed the red-faced men sitting on either side of the desk. "Only I thought it was time to go over to the Dancing School."

He stood in the doorway and wondered if he had only dreamed he had been invited to morning conference for the first time. He had heard so much about it.

He had risen early and studied that morning's edition of *The Pick Of The Crop.* He had even splashed out on a new pair of red and black bathers, which he carried in one hand. He had a beach towel slung over his shoulder.

"Ah, Norman?" the editor said. "Change of plans, I'm afraid. We're skipping the spa today."

"Oh?" Norman tried not to look disappointed.

"Come in anyway," Reg Collins said. "We're having our conference in here this morning."

The editor glared at the chief-of-staff. But before Dobber Leggs could protest, Norman had pulled up a chair.

"We'll continue this conversation later, Reginald." The editor stretched across the desk and took back his copy of the paper. He reached for a red marking pen from a jar. He flipped over the page and paused at the headline on Page Three.

Star dancer plans to waltz

away with premiership flag

A large photograph of Tiger Kowalski peered out from the page. Dobber Leggs scanned through the profile by Riley O'Reilly and his facial expressions changed from anger to amused approval.

One by one he flicked over the pages, pausing every now and then to scribble something.

When he came to the death notices, one name caught his eye. "So I was right? Gordon Rogers didn't look well."

"We've got his obituary in somewhere," the chief-of-staff said.

The editor looked puzzled. "I didn't see it."

"It's on Page Four," Norman said. "I wrote it."

The editor backtracked through the paper and found the obituary with a 36-point headline at the top of the page. "No wonder I missed it," he said. "Why couldn't we have put it on Page One?"

Norman knew why. Everyone in the office knew if a story was on Page One, the editor usually wanted to know why. If it wasn't on Page One, he usually wanted to know why not.

Dobber Leggs turned over some more pages and circled more stories. "Hmm, why haven't we got a follow-up on the hospital robbery?"

"We have," Reg Collins said. "It's on the bottom of Page Five."

"Page Five!" The editor looked up and scowled. "Don't you think it's worth a bit better than that?"

"You didn't think so yesterday."

"We had it on Page One yesterday!"

"Yes, but you didn't approve."

"I'd still like to know what's happening."

"Nothing is happening," Collins said. "The story says the police are at a dead end."

"What about the bikers in The Applecart? Did we bother to find out whether they were involved?"

"What makes you think they were involved?"

"It's all over town."

Norman interrupted. "I've heard that story, too, Mr Leggs. But it couldn't possibly be true. The bikers arrived after the incident at the hospital."

"What about the bikie laid up in the hospital then?" the editor said. "I hear he's been a patient for several days now. Could he be some kind of inside man?"

The chief-of-staff scratched his head. "If he is a forward scout, they're thinking well ahead. My recollection is the bikie in the hospital lives on Blackstump Road."

"Not another conservationist?" the editor said.

"I think he lives next door to the greenies; in the same house as Moose Routley. He's lived there for about three years."

"Three years?" The editor's voice went up. "Why haven't we had a story on him?"

"He doesn't seem to have done anything newsworthy," said Collins. "Moose is the bloke we should do a story on."

"Who's Moose?"

"Moose Routley, the footballer and Tasmanian Tiger hunter," Collins said. "We told you about him on Monday."

"Why haven't we written a story about him?"

"You said you weren't interested."

"Of course I'm interested. It's our job to be interested." He looked Norman in the eye. "You haven't lost interest in that feature story on the wind?"

"I'm still researching it, sir."

"Good boy. When will it be finished?"

"Soon," Norman said. Actually, he didn't have a clue.

The editor turned his attention back to the chief-of-staff. "What about the conservationists? Why didn't we have a story in about them today?"

"They were busy in a meeting every time we attempted to get them yesterday. So all we've got to go on is that vague press release they dropped into the office and I wouldn't touch that with a barge pole without verifying what they present as facts."

"What if they're planning something really big? For goodness sake, Reginald, make sure someone speaks to them today."

"Who? Apart from Michael Curtis, who's next to useless, I've only got three reporters rostered on and all of them are up to their eyeballs in work already."

"Curtis used to be a gun reporter when he was young and he had a decent chief-of-staff."

"You, you mean?"

"I had fewer reporters at my beck and call than you have now too."

Norman knew this was true. But in those days the paper came out twice a week, now it was five days a week.

"Curtis could still be a weapon in the right hands," the editor said. "Name me one reporter who writes a better book review? You've just got to be more selective with the work you assign."

Reg Collins made a fist and for an instant Norman thought he was going to reach over and punch the editor. But he placed both hands back flat on the desk, sat back in his chair, and looked up to the ceiling. "Every time I turn my head, you've given someone another story to do."

"I'm the editor."

"I'm supposed to be the one assigning the stories."

"Well, Reginald, I'm afraid you're not doing a very good job. Aside from notable absences of stories on the conservationists and this Moose Routley fellow, we didn't even have a story about the cow on Page Three today like we're supposed to."

"I'm not Mandrake."

"We've got to keep up our cow quota. We should be promoting her as much as possible. Have you got permission yet to take her on to the oval on Saturday?"

"I rang Oodles Noodle again but he still won't have a bar of it. He says the Mayor claims it's a public safety issue, and he's not going to budge."

"You'd better go see if you can talk some sense into James Northan."

"Me? Why me? You can do the secret handshake. Why can't you talk to him?"

"I haven't got time. I'm too busy doing your job already."

Collins opened his mouth to talk but no noise came out.

The editor clicked his fingers. "Norman, what are you up to today?"

"I was planning to go out looking for the wind, sir,"

"Who told you to do that?" Dobber Leggs glared at the chief-of-staff. "I want you to go see the conservationists on Blackstump Road. Find out what they're up to. Then I want you to track down this Moose Routley character and write a feature story on him."

"I'm not a football writer!"

"We want to know about his Tasmanian Tiger hunting too."

Norman nodded.

"One more thing," Dobber Leggs said. "When you return to town, go see the bikie in the hospital and find out what his story is." He clicked his fingers at the chief-of-staff. "Do you know his name, Reginald?"

"Foetus."

"Another Foetus?" Norman said. "What are the odds?"

———

MAYOR NORTHAN got angrier the longer the ring tone went on. Where was Oodles Noodle? *Ring-ring, ring-ring.* As he held the phone to his ear with his right hand, the Mayor looked at his watch. It was past 9 o'clock. Surely someone at the depot could hear the phone ringing?

It rang out.

How dare it!

All he wanted was for someone to swing by with a hammer and nails so they could hang his sign outside the council chambers. Was that too much to expect?

How dare Oodles and his men not be at work at this time of day! He ought to sack the lot of them.

Now he'd have to do it himself.

The problem was he didn't think he'd find the tools he needed around his office. He could send a junior to one of the stock and crop stores but he decided it would be quicker just to walk up the road himself.

Ten minutes later he was back at the council chambers, nailing a sign to the gate of the white picket fence that bordered the High Street. The fence was low to the ground but it was the only wooden surface in sight.

He was down on his knees, which was a very undignified pose for a Mayor in a pin-stripe suit.

The sign was neatly handwritten in thick, black letters on a large piece of white cardboard and said, **WANTED: ABLE-BODIED WORKMEN. TOP RATES. APPLY WITHIN.**

———

"CAPITALIST PIG," Sarah Sarandon muttered as the greenies walked past and saw the Mayor down on his knees sucking his thumb.

William looked at her sideways. It was as if she had been taking angry pills.

Sarah returned William's gaze with equal force. "Well, did you see him? Pitiful! Lucky for him he has so many fingers in so many pies he can probably afford to lose a few."

The greenies weren't normally out and about this early, but they were tramping to the general store to buy a newspaper to get some more ideas ahead of yet another meeting to decide how their protest should proceed.

"I wonder what all that's about?" William looked back over his shoulder but he was too far past the sign to be able to read the writing now.

"Who cares?" Dilly said.

When they bought their copy of the newspaper the sign made sense to them.

John held the paper as the others huddled around on the footpath outside the general store.

"This is terrible," William said. "Northan is trying to destroy the habitat of the Green Swift Parrot!"

"You still don't get it?" Dilly studied his face. "Nobody cares. We've moved on to the Tasmanian Tiger."

A look of delight came on to Sarah's face. It was probably the same look of delight Edison had when he had his lightbulb moment, or the one Lassiter got when he saw his golden reef. "Eureka!" she said.

———

SISTER Rowbottom was coming down the stairs when the bikers filed through the revolving door.

As they started climbing, she stretched out her arms and blocked their path.

"I don't understand." Foetus scratched the back of his neck. "We rang ahead."

"The bikie in room 15 is in no condition to leave with you."

Foetus's eyes widened. "The woman I spoke to on the phone told me the visiting hours. Clearly, though, you're not her. She had a sexy voice."

"I'm the head nurse, Sister Daisy Rowbottom. And I'm telling you, you're not taking him anywhere."

"Chill out sister. We just want to visit him, not take him with us.

He's not even a member of our gang. He couldn't ride with us, even if he wanted to."

This was true. This was more of a courtesy call. After two nights at The Applecart, Foetus thought they should drop in on a comrade and see if he needed cheering up.

The 18 male bikers and their six girlfriends left the hotel shortly before 10am. When they realised they were walking the wrong way, they crossed the road outside the council chambers, just short of the mayor's sign.

Mayor Northan saw them from his office window, and picked up the phone to warn Sergeant Birtwistle they were on the move. No answer. Typical!

Foetus studied the fat-arsed nurse blocking their path. He had to admire her courage. "Even if what you say is true, patients are limited to two visitors at a time," she said. "We can't have the lot of you traipsing into his room. I like to give my patients room to breathe."

Foetus offered his open palms. "OK, we'll choose a delegation to see him."

"Fine. But I don't want any trouble in my hospital. I'll know what's happened to him if he goes missing. And if you as much as look nasty to his roommate, I'm calling Sergeant Birtwistle."

The bikers backed down the stairs and stood in a huddle in the foyer as Foetus addressed them.

"Frizzle, you come with me. The rest of you can wait here. All except you, Bluey. You can go to the bakery and get 25 of those apple pies Wish-Wash raves about. We'll have one each for morning tea."

Foetus leant over and whispered in Bluey's ear. "Bring up mine and Frizzle's and one for the patient. But don't let that old bat see you. I have no doubt she'd call the cops if she knows more than two of us are up there and we're introducing tasty food to his bland hospital diet."

———

FOETUS was lying in bed trying to work out the best name for the newspaper's cow when the other two bikers burst into his room.

At first he thought the footsteps belonged to Bubby returning from his morning bath. But then he looked up to see leather and studs, beards and bandanas. The two strangers closed the door behind them and Foetus thought he was about to die.

But he realised the bigger of the visitors was just raising his hand for a high five. After an awkward pause, Foetus reached up and tagged it.

"Are you sure you've got the right patient?"

"Because we're from different gangs doesn't mean we have to be enemies," the visitor said. "I hear we share a name. I'm Foetus, this is Frizzle."

Another high five ensued.

"Us bikers have got to stick together in these hard times. We've heard all about you. Only a real Hells Angel would throw away the leather jacket he's made from animals he's killed with his bare hands so he can dare to wear those yellow pyjamas," the visiting Foetus said. "It tells the world you don't give a damn about what people think of you."

"Thanks." Foetus didn't know quite what to make of his guests and why they thought he was a Hells Angel. This didn't seem to be the right moment to fess up though. The misconception might be the only thing stopping them from smothering him with a pillow.

"Anything we can get you?"

"Some dope maybe?"

"Sorry," the other Foetus said. "We don't smoke the stuff. It's bad for you."

Foetus looked up at them and wondered if this was in fact some kind of weird dream. "What kinda bikers *are* you?"

"We're Aborigines," Frizzle said. His breath stank of garlic, and he balled his hands into fists. "You haven't got a problem with that?"

"Ah no. Of course not." Now didn't seem like the time to get all white supremacist. "How long are you blokes planning to stay in Windy Mountain?"

"Another day or two," the other Foetus said. "Longer if we can find work in the town."

"What kinda work are you looking for?"

"We'll do almost anything as long as it's legal."

This was getting weirder.

Frizzle sat down on the chair next to the bed, and his namesake stayed standing. They talked about places they had been, bikes they had ridden, and broken bones they had suffered.

The door creaked open and another bikie appeared carrying a paper bag.

The sick Foetus locked eyes with him and grinned broadly as recognition dawned on them both.

"Bluey?"

"Foetus?"

Foetus threw out his arms. "You carrot-top old bugger, I knew you'd come back for me!"

Bluey's face turned from pale to crimson. "Er, um, not exactly," he said as he moved towards the bed.

"What do you mean?"

"I'm just delivering the apple pies."

The other two bikers looked puzzled. "You two know each other?" asked Frizzle.

"Sure," the lying-down Foetus said. "Bluey and I ride together in the same gang."

Bluey's words came out slow and hesitant. "I thought you would have heard? I'm a Muttonbird now."

Garlic Breath's face twisted. "Bluey, I didn't know you used to be a Hells Angel?"

Bluey handed out the pies. "No, Foetus and I were members of The Thunderbirds."

"I thought Foetus was a Hells Angel?" Frizzle said.

Time to own up. PJs Foetus forced a laugh. "No, there's been some kind of misunderstanding."

Bluey cleared his throat. "Didn't you know? The Thunderbirds disbanded?"

"What?"

The other Foetus nodded. "When they folded, Bluey transferred to The Muttonbirds."

"Transferred? We're bikers, not footballers. Once a Thunderbird, always a Thunderbird. We can't disband — and we don't have fucking transfers."

"The recession changed all that," Bluey said. "Strong gangs survived and weak gangs folded."

It was a good thing Foetus was already lying down. "I don't believe it," he gasped. "I've been waiting all this time for The Thunderbirds to come back for me!" He could hear blood swishing into his cranium.

Bluey hung his head. "The bank repossessed most of our bikes."

"The bastards." Foetus tossed his head aside so the others couldn't see the tears welling up in his eyes. "Just tell me one thing, Bluey? Why did you and the blokes leave me here?"

"It was meant to be a joke."

"A joke!" Foetus found full voice again and brushed away his tears. "When did you plan to return?"

"In a couple of hours. But we had a bit of trouble remembering exactly where we had left you. All these little towns look so much alike." He paused. "If I had known you were here in hospital I would have come to see you earlier."

"I heard you arrive *two days ago*!"

"But I didn't know you were here. Honestly!"

"You must have gotten a bit of a clue when you heard a bikie named Foetus was in the hospital?"

"No, why would I?" Bluey said. "Do you know how many bikers called Foetus I know?"

"But I was the only Foetus in The Thunderbirds."

The other Foetus came to Bluey's rescue. "Wish-Wash didn't tell us you were one of The Thunderbirds. He must have got mixed up when he told us you were a Hells Angel."

———

A TALL woman with straggly hair answered the door of the Brian Jacobs Memorial Commune before Norman J. Hit even had the chance to knock. He figured she must have heard him skid to a halt on the gravel road.

"Um, good morning." Norman was taken aback when the door opened. "I'm a reporter from *The Pick Of The Crop* newspaper."

"How many trees died to produce today's edition?"

Norman's face creased. "I need to talk to whoever's in charge?"

"We have one bloke who *thinks* he's in charge." She flicked her hair back. "But the person you really need is Sarah. I'll get her."

She disappeared inside, leaving Norman fumbling with his notebook and tape recorder for several minutes. He could hear voices but he couldn't hear what they were saying. Finally a blonde woman with tied-back hair appeared.

"I'm Sarah Sarandon," she said. "Won't you come in? We've got a press statement to make."

They drank herbal tea at the big wooden table in the kitchen and Norman listened, took notes and asked questions. Pretty soon he knew it had the makings of a big story. The greenie also armed him with some interesting information for his next stop.

———

AS THE morning wore on, Mayor Northan became more anxious. Not one person applied for a job. His sign had been defaced, passers-by had made rude gestures towards him through the window of his office and one old fruit-grower had even spat on the footpath in full knowledge he was watching.

When Birty called by about 11am, the Mayor had worked himself into a state.

"I told you no one in this town is going to help you tear down that orchard."

"Why not?"

The policeman rolled his eyes. "You haven't even got council approval."

"I don't need council approval. It's a private orchard."

"Why did you try to get approval at the council meeting last night then?"

"I would have got it too if it wasn't for Bumface leading a revolt against me. If you can't get him for treason, I'm sure you can lock him up for the lifestyle he leads."

Birty fixed his eyes on him.

"Well, it stands to reason. Man of his age still unmarried? Can't you put a bug in his house, get conclusive evidence?"

Birty rolled his eyes again. Tasmania still had anti-homosexuality laws but they were not vigilantly enforced.

"Anyway, I only took the matter to council as a courtesy. What happened doesn't change a thing. I don't think any court in the land would bar me from getting rid of my own orchard."

"Looks like you'll have to do it on your own then, Mr Mayor."

"I'll get my workforce, you'll see."

"Don't expect the police to save you if things get out of hand."

"How could things possibly get out of hand?"

"I've seen these types of situations before. Things can get nasty."

The Mayor snapped. "It's really none of your business. If you spent as much time trying to fight crime . . ." his voice trailed off and he waggled a finger. "Have you solved the hospital robbery yet? I rang earlier to tell you the bikers were on the move and you obviously couldn't be bothered to pick up the phone."

———

"ME?" Moose said as the reporter followed him into a storage shed. "Why would anyone be interested in me?"

"You're being modest," Norman J. Hit said. "Football star, Tasmanian Tiger hunter . . ."

Moose picked up a metal cage, and started walking away. "I'm sorry, mate. But I'm not interested in being interviewed."

Norman caught up to him. "Don't you think you owe it to your many fans? A lot of our readers would like to know more about you."

"Look." Moose stopped. "It's nothing personal. I don't give interviews. As a footballer, I'm just part of the team. And as a Tasmanian Tiger hunter, I want to keep a low profile."

Norman put his hands on his hips.

"Even if you refuse to talk to me, I'm still going to have to write about you. My editor will insist on it. I'd prefer your input so I don't get the facts wrong."

Moose grinned. "I've never met a reporter yet who's got the facts right."

"Trust me."

"Why should I?"

Norman didn't want to play his trump card, but he felt he had to. He had never done anything like this before in his short career. But this was a big story. "Because if you don't trust me, I am going to expose you as a thief."

"What?" Moose dropped the cage and it landed with a thud.

"I know all about the firewood you steal from the Brian Jacobs Memorial Commune."

"You're not serious?"

"Oh yes I am." Norman slipped in a fib. "I've got photographs too."

Moose tore at his hair.

"I don't believe you. These photos don't exist, it's impossible."

Norman turned to leave. "Have it your own way. I'll send you a copy of the paper."

He got all the way to the front gate when Moose called him back.

———

MAYOR Northan welcomed Reg Collins into his office like an old friend. "Sit down. You've come about the job, have you?"

"What job?"

The Mayor sat down behind his desk. "You must have seen my sign outside?"

"Oh that?" Collins smiled. "No, I'm not interested in that. I'm from *The Pick Of The Crop*. I'm here about the cow."

"What cow?"

"I thought you knew all about it? Oodles reckons he was acting on your orders."

"Oh, that. Are you a reporter here to do a story?"

"No, I'm the newspaper's chief-of-staff. Reg Collins."

The Mayor hissed, "You're the fool who hired that Sydney journalist!"

Before Collins could defend himself, the Mayor continued his tirade.

"Frankly, Mr Collins, I think you've got a cheek. You hire some journalistic cowboy from Sydney, your newspaper glorifies common criminals, you defame me . . . and now you want *my* help."

Collins folded his arms. "It's just a cow." He tried to appeal to the Mayor's vanity. "We'd be happy for you to pose with her for a photo."

"You seriously want me to endanger the lives of the players in the grand final by allowing cow doo-doo to be left on the ground? Do you have any idea about the public liability claims we might be exposing ourselves to?"

"We'd be careful. We'd get the copyboy to walk behind with a big pooper-scooper."

"You hold me up to public ridicule, you tell lies about me . . . what don't you understand about the word no?"

The Mayor stood up and pointed to the door.

———

MOOSE and Norman sat down in the kitchen. "I really can't talk about some things."

Norman was adjusting the tape-recorder he had placed on the table.

"Some of the things I do are pretty touchy." Moose looked at what Norman was doing with his hands. "You haven't switched that thing on yet?"

"No, see." Norman pointed to the play button that was still in the off position.

"This is definitely not for publication, but if the authorities read I'm trying to catch a Tasmanian Tiger in a cage they might not be too happy with me."

"Why not?"

"It's taboo to actually catch a Tasmanian Tiger. But it's Catch 22: If you can't catch one, you can't prove it exists. You can come up with all the photographs you like and the doubters will cry *trick photography*. I've found a couple of scats in the bush I reckon must have come from Tasmanian Tigers, but that's not enough to satisfy the wildlife officials. So I've got no choice but to try to catch one in a cage. A live Thylacine is the only real proof there is. Even a dead one is no proof any others are alive."

"You really don't have to worry about me. I'm not one of those tabloid reporters.'

"And you won't mention that, er, um, other little thing either?"

"I told you, you can trust me.'

Norman started the tape recorder.

"Have you actually seen a Tasmanian Tiger yet?"

Moose reached over and turned the recorder off. "You can't really expect me to answer that! Poor old Wish-Wash lost all his credibility when he claimed he had seen a Tasmanian Tiger. Who's going to take seriously a Tasmanian Tiger hunter who says he hasn't seen one? This is my livelihood, mate, and it's in my professional interests to keep people guessing."

"What do you say in response to the greenies up the road who claim they've seen Tasmanian Tigers in the Northan apple orchard?"

"They reckon what?" Moose threw out his hands.

"I was speaking to . . ." — Norman flicked through his notebook, which was on the table — ". . . Sarah Sarandon. She said they've seen Tasmanian Tigers among the apple trees."

Moose shook his head. "I think she must have been pulling your leg, mate. Tasmanian Tigers are shy animals. No way they'd live anywhere near that orchard. How can you believe anything those people say? Greenies always have ulterior motives. I suppose it was them who told you about me and their woodshed too?"

Norman avoided Moose's gaze. He clicked the tape on again.

"Can you tell me something about your hunting routine?"

"I'd rather not reveal the exact location but can tell you I've pinpointed a certain area as the most likely habitat. It's not too far away from here, but I usually camp out overnight."

"Are you nervous about playing in the grand final?"

"I'm doing my best to keep it out of my mind. I'm going out hunting this afternoon, I always find that's a good distraction. I'll be back home before lunch, and we've got our final training session tomorrow night."

"Are you looking forward to the parade on Friday?"

Moose studied him. "Are you serious! What parade?"

"The grand final parade down the main street."

Moose's face went pale. "I don't know anything about any parade."

"You must know about it." Norman explained how it was a tradition on the rare occasion the Tigers made the grand final. A parade was held in the High Street the night before the match and the mayor introduced the players to the crowd from the balcony at the Dancing School. The whole town was expected to line the streets.

Moose spoke to the air above Norman's head. "When were they going to tell me?"

————

NORMAN still wanted to talk to some of Moose's associates to gather some background for his story.

Over the next hour, he interviewed Hoo-Chung Loo, Tiger Kowalski and Wee Jimmy McMartin. He had no idea what the Scottish baker actually said.

Then he visited the Windy Mountain Hospital.

"I've got nothing to say," Foetus said. "What Moose does is his own business."

"I'm not trying to paint Moose in a bad light. I'm just trying to build up a profile on the man."

"Does Moose know you're writing a story about him?"

"I interviewed him today."

"Moose doesn't give interviews."

"He changed his mind."

Foetus looked suspicious. "Who else have you talked to about him?"

"Some of his team-mates."

"What do you need me for then?"

"You live with him," Norman said. "Maybe you've noticed things about him others haven't."

"Like what?"

"I got the impression he isn't exactly looking forward to the grand final parade on Friday?"

"What parade?"

"Not you, too?" Norman nodded towards the glass door that led to the balcony. "You'll probably get a good view from here."

"Moose has never mentioned any parade. Are you sure he even knows?"

"I told him."

Foetus crossed his arms. "I told you, I've got nothing to say about Moose."

"OK," Norman said. "What about you then? Can I ask you about the robbery here the other day?"

"I can't tell you anything that hasn't already been in your own rag.

They didn't come near me. I've already told the police that."

Norman looked Foetus in the eye. "A rumour going around town has it the bikers in The Applecart may have had something to do with the robbery."

"I wouldn't know about that."

"I've heard suggestions you might be a member of that gang."

"Me?" Foetus said. "Here we go again!"

———

MAYOR Northan was getting desperate. It was 2.30pm and no one had responded to the sign.

He rang Tiger Kowalski at the Dancing School and asked if the football team might be interested in an extra workout. "For money, of course," he added. But Tiger knew what it was all about, the whole town knew. "Sorry, we've got a premiership to win."

Mayor Northan walked to the works depot to find Oodles. Maybe he and his men were interested in doing a bit of moonlighting? But Oodles knew what the Mayor was up to, too, and had warned members of his staff. No one was interested.

When Mayor Northan saw Johnno and The Big O painting the boundary fence around the football oval, he strolled over. "You two men wouldn't be interested in a little extra work, would you?"

"You'd be the Mayor, dat right?" The Big O said.

"Yeeees." Mayor Northan looked down on The Big O with disdain as soon as he heard the accent. "Do I know you?"

"I used to be the local Catholic priest."

All Mayor Northan could imagine in front of him was an ill-educated man dressed in a canvas tunic covered in arrows with his ankle chained to a heavy metal ball.

"I read about you in the newspaper today," The Big O said. "You want to tear down your orchard."

"I'm offering good money to anyone who cares to help me."

"You can keep your money as far as we're concerned. isn't dat right, Johnno?"

Mayor Northan turned to go away. "Good day to you, gentlemen," he said curtly.

He was running out of options. He thought about trying The Applecart until he remembered The Muttonbirds were holed up there. Well, they had been. Everyone in town knew they had gone en masse to visit the bikie in the hospital, which added flesh to the bones of Mayor Northan's theory of how the Great Sperm Robbery had been pulled off. Probably they were back at the pub now, though.

Mayor Northan drove his car to the outskirts of town to visit old Mrs Nancy Browning, who was chief co-ordinator of the Anglican Church volunteer working bee which was made up of senior citizens. She fed him on tea and cake, but was no help at all. "We're too frail," she said. "Besides, we don't want to see that orchard disappear. It means a lot to us old people."

Mayor Northan was flabbergasted.

Surely, in these days of widespread unemployment, someone must be willing to help him? It was only a silly old orchard, for goodness sake.

He returned to his office and rang the Commonwealth Employment Office in Launceston. They said they could raise a workforce, but would need two weeks. "I haven't got two weeks," Mayor Northan cried. "I want it done tomorrow."

He rang the Army Reserve but they said they only got together at weekends, unless a war broke out.

He even rang around a few members of his Masonic Lodge, but most of them just laughed at him.

———

REG Collins went to see Tiger Kowalski to put in a plea for *The Pick Of The Crop's* cow. "You've got some influence with the Mayor. Can you help me?"

"I doubt it," Tiger said. "I really appreciate what you and the news-paper are doing to promote the grand final. But you know the Mayor? Once his mind is made up . . ."

Reg Collins was turning to leave when Tiger spoke again.

But it was a short-lived glimmer of hope. "Oh Reg, will you be using the spa tomorrow morning?"

Collins turned. "Yes, I think so. We had a bit of a hiccup in our routine this morning but things should be back to normal tomorrow."

"Good, I hate to see a Silver Pass going to waste."

———

THE jukebox was between songs when a *tap, tap, tap* came at the door.

It was nearly 11pm. Frizzle went to check who'd be dropping in at this time of night.

He switched on the external light and opened the door. The shivering man at the top of the steps said, "I've come to put a business proposition to you and your companions."

Frizzle had to chew though and swallow his garlic mountain oyster before he could speak. "Do you know what time it is?" He looked left and right, then blew out a stream of garlic breath, which formed a cloud in the cold night air. "I suppose you'd better come in then."

Mayor Northan stepped up into the doorway, but the bikie didn't appear to get much shorter.

The Mayor had stood outside for two hours trying to pluck up the courage to knock. It was hard to tell whether his shivering came from the cold or fear of what waited for him inside.

The afternoon hadn't yielded any joy at all. Mayor Northan had rung several business contacts in neighbouring towns trying to enlist workmen. But word of his plans had travelled quickly and no one wanted anything to do with him. He tried to place a Positions Vacant advertisement with *The Pick Of The Crop* but the girls at the front counter refused to accept it. By nightfall, he was a tired and beaten man, and now it had come to this.

The Mayor started removing his coat as he followed the bikie up the passage into the noisy, smoke-filled bar. He had never seen so many tattooed forearms and bearded faces in one spot. Artie Rogerson was pouring ciders and Wish-Wash was sitting on a stool at the bar talking to two bikers who looked transfixed by what he was telling them. A strange version of *Shaddup Ya Face* was playing on the jukebox in the corner. It wasn't Joe Dolce, but Mayor Northan recognised the voice as belonging to Manuel, the waiter from that dreadful show *Fawlty Towers*.

Frizzle pointed out Foetus, who was sitting at a table playing cards. "You'd better go talk to the boss."

With his cashmere coat folded over his right arm, Mayor Northan walked over to Foetus and held out his hand. "Hello, sir, I'm Mayor James Northan. I've come to, er, um, welcome you and see if you and your people are interested in picking up a little pocket money?"

Foetus put his cards face down on the table. "Wish-Wash said you wouldn't have the balls to come near this place. Yet here you are." Foetus gave Mayor Northan's hand a low-slung high-five slap. "Mind if I call you, Jimbo? Everyone calls *me* Foetus . . . except my mum."

Foetus clicked his fingers towards the bar. "Another cider for the Mayor, thanks Rog."

Mayor Northan raised a palm. "Oh, not for me, thank you very much. I only popped by quickly to see if you're interested in doing a small job for me. I'm driving."

Foetus dragged a chair from the next table and motioned for the Mayor to sit down. "One little drink won't put you over the limit. You do play Poker?"

Bridge was the Mayor's only card game and he normally only drank top shelf. But when a large glass of cider was placed on the table, he forced himself to smile.

"I suppose just one will be all right." He hung his coat carefully on the back of the chair and sat down. "I'll have to pass on the card game though. I really did only pop in to put a business proposition to you."

"What's the rush?" Foetus took a huge gulp of his cider, then wiped some of the froth from his beard. He called over other bikers.

"You've met Frizzle." The Mayor extended his hand again, only to get another low-slung high five. "And this is Bluey . . . this is Seagull . . . this is Micky . . . and Janine." Even *her* high-five hurt. Foetus winked at Janine. "You sure you don't want to play cards, Jimbo? Janine plays a mean game of Strip Poker."

Then he introduced the bikers already sitting at the table, Skull, Rooter and another Foetus. "Now these are blokes you ought not take your clothes off for."

Mayor Northan smiled. That was a joke, right?

"And you know Wish-Wash?" Foetus nodded to the next chair.

That was a shock. Mayor Northan hadn't seen the former town drunk leave his stool, but he was now sitting next to him, and he acknowledged him with a lukewarm nod of his head. But no way was he going to high-five that cretin.

The Mayor turned to face the head bikie again. "What have you found out about our little town?" He was actually fishing for information that would inform the way he had to proceed. If The Muttonbirds knew anything about the plans he had for his orchard and the emotions the proposal had stirred up, he knew he'd need to do some fancy footwork.

"This pub is great," Foetus said. "Never heard the likes of this juke-box. It's got all different versions of the same song. Who knew an Aboriginal version of *Shaddup Ya Face* existed?" He looked towards the jukebox. "Like it? This is Gnarnayarrahe Waitairie's version that just started now. Bet you never expected to hear the Indjibundji language in this town."

Mayor Northan nodded weakly. He hoped Whish-Willson hadn't told the bikers he had moved a motion at council to force the hotel to change the music on that jukebox. Had Bumface not led a revolt, they'd be listening to Bach or Beethoven right now.

"Wish-Wash has told us all about the town." Foetus smiled, which revealed his missing teeth.

"I hope you don't believe everything he has said?" Mayor Northan laughed nervously.

"Nah, we're not that gullible." Foetus pointed to a bowl of mountain oysters on another table and laughed. "Wish-Wash told us those things are sheep's balls!"

"Ah! Well, er, um, they actually are."

Foetus screwed up his face as if he was in pain. "I've already eaten about three dozen of them."

"They're supposed to do wonders for the libido."

"It's the poor old rams' libidos I'm worried about."

Mayor Northan smiled weakly. "You didn't happen to see the local newspaper today by any chance?"

"No, but we saw it yesterday. Wish-Wash reckons the article about us was the best story he's seen in the paper since he was last interviewed."

"Really?" The Mayor glanced sideways, only to realise Whish-Willson had gone back to his stool. How was he to know the jukebox would suddenly stop and everyone in the bar would hear him laugh and say, "He's told you about the Tasmanian Tiger he saw strolling up the High Street then?"

"Yes, I did," Wish-Wash said. "And The Muttonbirds believed me too."

Frizzle added his outrage. "What's wrong with you people? Wish-Wash should be one of the town's icons."

Everyone was looking at the Mayor. The only noise he could hear was his heartbeat. "Wish-Wash is my friend." He looked over to the former town drunk, pleading for his support.

"Are you sure?" Frizzle said. "Cause it doesn't look that way to me. You didn't even high-five him."

Mayor Northan got up, walked over to Whish-Willson and awkwardly put his arm around him. "Wish-Wash and I are like brothers. Aren't we, mate?" It was the first time he had ever used the man's nickname and he hoped the word *mate* didn't sound too forced. It wasn't a word he often used unless he was commenting on TV nature shows.

"What do you think about his Tasmanian Tiger then?" Bluey's glare burnt into him.

"I believe every word he said." Mayor Northan held up his palm for a high five. "Don't I, um, Wish-Wash?"

Wish-Wash tagged him but said nothing. He looked like he was in a state of shock.

Mayor Northan cleared his throat. "About this job I have? I read you fellows are looking for work in Windy Mountain?"

"That's right," Foetus said. "How many of us are you interested in hiring?"

"All of you."

"What kind of work is it?" Seagull asked.

"I can't divulge that right now."

"Why not?" Foetus's face darkened. "It's nothing illegal, is it?"

"Um, no-ooo." Mayor Northan made the word into two syllables. "This job is more or less in the demolition field. Being bikers, I'm sure you'll enjoy it."

Foetus beckoned the Mayor back to his table with a come-hither index finger.

Foetus drew his face menacingly close to the Mayor's "We're bikers; not criminals. We hate violence, we hate illicit drugs and we prefer to build things than wreck them." He tapped the Mayor three times on the chest with his huge finger to punctuate his last words. "Is that clear?"

"See that bloke?" Foetus pointed to a large figure hunched over the jukebox trying to pick out another *Shaddup Ya Face* song. "Brutus is a scientist. And see him?" Foetus pointed again. "Frizzle is a bank manager. Bluey over there works as a field officer for the Aboriginal and Torres Strait Islander Commission. And Shazza over there is a commercial artist."

"I'm a parole officer," Foetus said. "And I don't take shit from anyone. OK?"

Mayor Northan could feel his Adam's apple bob as he gulped.

"I suppose you want to know why people of our social standing are riding motorbikes around the countryside?"

"It hadn't crossed my mind."

"I'll tell you anyway." Foetus broke into another toothless smile. "We're all on holidays, see."

"Oh?"

"Yeah, and we like to pick up work to help make our holiday pay go further. But it has to be legal."

"It is. Honestly."

"So can't you even give us a hint what you want us to do for you?"

Mayor Northan thought for a moment, cupped his hand around his mouth and whispered into Foetus's ear. "Apples."

THIRTEEN
GREENIES ENTER THE FRAY

MAYOR NORTHAN DIDN'T OFTEN HUM a happy tune. But he even had a skip in his step when he crossed his front lawn early the next morning. He couldn't wait to see what had been written in *The Pick of the Crop*.

He had nearly missed the newspaper's deadline. But when he finally got away from the pub close to midnight, he had rung and told them to *stop the presses*.

It gave him great pleasure to be able to tell Norman J. Hit he had delivered on his promise to secure a workforce to rip out his orchard.

"Who's got egg on their faces now?" he said to himself as he rolled back the rubber band and held the newspaper up to the garden light. It was a bit slippery underfoot after some overnight rain but it looked like the weather had cleared.

His eyes nearly popped out as he scanned the front page.

GREENIES VOW TO SAVE TIGERS' HOME
> **Battle looms at orchard as**
> **Mayor hires workforce**

. . .

By Norman J. Hit

FOUR conservationists are set to clash with workmen in a battle over a Windy Mountain apple orchard which the greenies say is home to a family of Tasmanian Tigers.

The conservationists say they have seen Tasmanian Tigers nesting under trees at the Northan apple orchard.

They say they will form a blockade at the site to prevent anyone from destroying the orchard.

The owner, Mayor James Northan, sparked a walkout at the Windy Mountain Council on Tuesday night when he sought permission to rip out the historic trees to make way for a windsock factory. He was adamant late last night he would go ahead with his plans. He even claimed to have hired a secret workforce.

But a spokesman for the conservationists, Sarah Sarandon, said, "We will not rest until we have thwarted the Mayor's sinister plans.

"We believe the Tasmanian Tiger is not extinct. It is, in fact, living in Windy Mountain and is in mortal danger."

Mayor Northan wasn't aware he was making noises in the front garden, but he must have been because next thing he knew his wife was calling out and asking what the problem was.

"Coming, dear." He kicked Kipling, the family's little white dog. Served him right for being under his feet.

When he got to the door, Mayor Northan thrust the paper at Prue.

She glanced at the front page to see what all the fuss was about, then she sat down at the other end of the table, sub-divided the paper to give the front to their teenage daughter Maddie, and grabbed her pen.

If she had looked up from her crossword, she might have thought James was frothing at the mouth as he ate his cereal. But actually it was mainly milk dribbling down his chin.

After a period of simmering silence, he cried, "I'll sue, I'll sue," as he spat flakes and saliva all over the kitchen table.

"Who are you going to sue this time, dear?" Prue still didn't look up.

"The conservationists, the newspaper, everyone. No Tasmanian Tigers live in my orchard. These are lies, filthy rotten lies aimed at preventing me from making money." His voice got louder with every word.

Prue put the paper down, got up and walked over to the toaster. "People have been claiming to have seen the Tasmanian Tiger for years. Maybe the greenies' sighting is genuine?"

"If Tasmanian Tigers did live in my orchard don't you think I'd know!"

In a more modest house nearby, Sergeant Birtwistle was equally distraught when he read the newspaper story. "Blinking greenies. Blinking Tasmanian Tigers. Blinking Mayor. Blinking newspaper."

Coming on top of The Great Sperm Robbery, it was the last thing he needed in the dwindling days of his career.

If Wish-Wash had seen the article, he would have felt vindicated. But he didn't.

The reason for this was he was still asleep. At Mayor Northan's suggestion, he had bunked down with The Muttonbirds in an apple storage shed off the High Street.

But who knew it was going to be so cold overnight? Wish-Wash had gone back to the pub to see if Rog had any warm blankets he could spare. Rog shook his head but he pointed his broom to the back of a nearby chair. "Someone left their coat. Why don't you take that to cover yourself with?"

———

NORMAN J. HIT felt awful. It wasn't the raindrops on the tin roof that had kept him awake for most of the night. When he stooped down to pick up his newspaper from the still-dark front lawn, he knew which of his stories he'd regret most.

He unfurled the paper, and flicked straight to Page Three to confirm what he had already replayed in his mind over and over as he had tossed and turned.

The faulty light on the street made clicking noises as it flickered, but its strobe light effect still provided all the illumination he needed to see the page.

The report was a far cry from Norman's first attempt. He had written a profile that betrayed no secrets, and he had taken the story over to the night editor's desk.

But Sean McWhirter took one look at it and his face exploded with rage.

"What is this piece of shit!" He tore Norman's 12 sheets of copy paper into about 112 pieces and threw them into his wastepaper basket. "Sit back down and have another go at it. I want it longer and I want it stronger for Page Three."

Norman retreated to his desk. He grabbed a sheet of copy paper and fed it roughly into the typewriter. *Stronger? I'll give him stronger.*

In hindsight, Norman knew he should have stood his ground. He stared at the story in horror as he stood next to his hedge. The headline McWhirter had written made it seem even worse.

TOP TIGER TALKS EXCLUSIVELY TO *THE PICK OF THE CROP*:
Wood thief has stage-fright!
Nobody told me I'd have to be in a grand final parade, says Moose.

He flicked back to Page One. He knew the Mayor wouldn't be happy but it might have helped if he had phoned earlier, which would have given Norman more time to tweak the article he had already written.

———

SARAH Sarandon squinted at a sign on the fence which said, 'Northan Apples Pty Ltd. Trespassers will be prosecuted.'

The four conservationists had walked in darkness from Blackstump Road. Sarah had traded her high heels for sneakers and her bright clothes for something darker and less glamorous. She carried bolt-cutters, William marched like a reluctant soldier going into battle, and John and Dilly struggled to keep up because they carried either end of a big canvas bag.

The overnight rain had left puddles and given way to a bitterly cold south-westerly wind.

William screwed up his face when he looked into the darkness. "I can't see any Tasmanian Tigers. I can't even see any apple trees in this light."

Sarah glared. 'All will be revealed when the sun rises."

"You won't see apples, that's for sure," William said. "It's too early in the season for apples. So even if Tasmanian Tigers do eat fruit, which I very much doubt, why would they even be here?"

Sarah adjusted her beanie then snipped the chain across the access road.

While John and Dilly gathered some twigs and dead branches and started a small campfire, Sarah unfurled a banner which she strung between two trees. All William did was stand and watch.

He laughed when he saw the words on the banner, THE TASSIE TIGER LIVES, OK? He was less amused when Sarah dug into the big bag and pulled out the hand-held placards from their protest at the commune; the words *Green Swift Parrot* had been scribbled out and replaced with *Thylacine*.

When the fire was lit, the four greenies sat around and warmed their hands. William looked into the embers. "How long do we have to sit here?"

"Until someone comes," Sarah said.

———

"WHAT is this flapdoodle!" Dobber Leggs slammed a fist down on the water. He and Reg Collins were alone in the spa. "Why haven't you fired that fool?"

"I asked him yesterday afternoon if he would resign and he said no. What else can I do? Do we really want to risk angering the union? Besides, what if the greenies are right? What if the story is quite legitimate?"

"I can't believe you just said that. Truth has got nothing to do with it. Do you honestly believe James Northan deserves to have his business scuttled in this way?"

"You heard about the sign he put up yesterday? it's quite clear he wants to destroy that orchard."

"But that doesn't mean this newspaper has to give credibility to some cock-and-bull story by the conservationists about Tasmanian Tigers living there."

"Yes, but what if Tasmanian Tigers really do live in the orchard?"

The editor smashed his hand down on the water again, sending more splatters of water flying. "Is it any wonder I don't want young reporters joining us for conference any more? I'd like to protect them from warped thoughts like that? You know as well as I do conservationists have a track record for coming up with these types of stunts. Now a fine upstanding citizen who just happens to be Mayor wants to remove an unprofitable orchard, they reckon they've found the home of the Tasmanian Tiger — something none of the rest of us have been able to corner for the past 50 years!"

"Wish-Wash did," Reg Collins said. "The national media believed him too. Imagine the field day they'll have this time?"

"Their reputations aren't on the line. When they've gone home, we're the ones who have to regain the respect of the community." The editor paused and then said, "Anyway, I blame you for this. You should never have sent out a gullible, inexperienced reporter to interview the greenies."

Collins let that comment go. "We've got another problem."

"Oh spare me!"

"I went to see Mayor Northan yesterday, and he's still adamant he doesn't want the cow on the football ground at halftime."

————

MAYOR Northan slid open the door to his apple storage shed.

All he could hear was a chorus of snoring. As his eyes adjusted, he saw sleeping people all over the concrete floor.

"Foetus, Foetus." The Mayor whispered as he stepped over bodies. "Are you here?"

A leather bundle nearby groaned, and Mayor Northan stepped towards it.

"Foetus, is that you?"

Foetus slowly lifted his head up and squinted towards the light beaming through the open door, then tried to focus on the figure above him.

"What time is it?"

"Nine-thirty."

The leader of the pack sat up and rubbed his eyes. "I only got to bed a few hours ago. I told you last night, we're on our holidays."

"Slight change of plans. We need to get you lot out of here because I forgot we need to use this warehouse today."

This wasn't true. The real reason was he needed to ensure none of the bikers laid their eyes on that day's newspaper.

The article in *The Pick Of The Crop* probably wasn't as damning as he first thought. Perhaps it would even swing public opinion his way. He thought most decent folk hated conservationists, because these lowlifes had a reputation of being anti-employment. But Mayor Northan didn't want to take any chances.

"You want us to go to work now!" Foetus got to his feet.

"No, not now. Tonight."

Some of the other bikers were wide awake now; most of the others were stirring.

Foetus looked into the mayor's eyes. "If we can't stay here, what do you plan to do with us until tonight, Jimbo?"

"I thought you might like to go on a bus tour."

"But all our gear is here?"

"That's OK," the Mayor said. "We'll work around it. Everything will be safe."

"Where are you going to get a bus from anyway?"

"I've got a work bus."

"Can Wish-Wash come too?"

"Sure he can." In fact, Mayor Northan had been banking on it. He didn't want *anyone* in the group to know what awaited them at the orchard. He looked around the room hoping to catch sight of Whish-Willson. He saw his cashmere coat first, then the familiar stubbled face bob up from under it.

"That's my ... that's my ..." He couldn't quite get out the words.

"What's wrong?" Foetus said.

Mayor Northan felt sick. He now realised in his haste to leave the pub he had forgotten to take his coat. That coat had been a gift to him from a visiting Japanese wool baron whose fine textiles graced the catwalks of Milan. Mr Fukisumo had sourced the cashmere from a finer-than-fine goat-herd in South America. And somehow Whish-Willson had now got it. Even if he could get it back, he'd have to get it fumigated.

He swallowed some foul air. "I'm just so happy to see my mate," he forced himself to say.

Foetus scratched his forehead. "Have you got a driver for this tour?"

"I thought one of you might like to drive."

"How do you know you can trust us with your bus?"

"I'll be with you."

———

BIRTY tried to give Junior Constable Stretch a crash course in restraint and diplomacy. "Who knows what will happen when the greenies meet Mayor Northan's workforce."

"I didn't know Mayor Northan even had a workforce?"

"Neither did I until I read *The Pick Of The Crop* this morning."

It was 9.45am. Stretch stood in front of Birty's desk. Stretch's shirt was freshly starched and his black leather shoes were finely polished. A pair of handcuffs hung from his belt.

"This is a very sensitive situation," the sergeant cautioned. "I want you to use your common sense, give everyone a little bit of leeway."

"You can rely on me, sarge."

"I've already been out to the orchard to see what's happening. The greenies set up a blockade at dawn but Mayor Northan's workforce was nowhere in sight."

"Do we know when they're even going to arrive?"

"No, but we'll go out there together next time. I've asked the District Superintendent to put reinforcements on standby in case things get out of hand. At this stage, though, all I want is for us to visit the protest site at least every hour to let them know we are watching. I've got Smithy starting work at 7pm to cover the nightshift."

Stretch drew a deep breath. "Are Tasmanian Tigers really living in that orchard?"

The sergeant smiled. "I've lived in this town for 33 years and I haven't seen one yet."

"Didn't the bloke they call Wish-Wash say he has?"

"And look where it's got him?"

———

THE PENNY dropped for Johnno when he saw the bikers and Wish-Wash crossing to the toilet blocks on the other side of the footy oval.

He and The Big O were just coming around the flank.

The Big O looked over to Mayor Northan's storage shed from

where the bikers had come. "The Mayor would be furious if he knew they had slept dare last night."

"Unless," Johnno said, "he was the one who gave them the key."

"What are you saying?" The Big O squinted towards another procession of bikers.

"It figures. We know he's hired himself some workers to tear down his orchard. What if the bikers are the ones? No one else in this town would be ill-informed enough to sign up."

"I don't tink even the Mayor would stoop dat low. Would he?"

"One way to find out," Johnno said. "We'll have to go to the orchard."

"When?"

Johnno shrugged. "Tonight, I guess. The Tasmanian Tiger is nocturnal so if it really lives in that orchard night-time will be the best time to see it."

"Don't tell me you believe the greenies?"

"Why would they make the story up?"

"You're the assistant Tasmanian Tiger hunter here. What do you tink?"

Johnno pondered for a moment then said, "Moose and I have never actually searched in that orchard area before."

———

THE EYES of the Australian media fell quickly on Windy Mountain. The Tasmanian Tiger always makes good copy, and word spread like bushfire. When the editors of the bigger Tasmanian newspapers heard, they despatched reporters and photographers to the scene. Tasmanian television stations weren't far behind. By 10am, journalists and technical staff from all the national television networks were on their way to Windy Mountain. By lunchtime, five television crews and eight newspaper representatives were at the protest site looking for the best angle on the story. *The Pick Of The Crop* was represented by Michael Curtis, who had brought with him a novel he was reviewing.

Councillors Peter Rowbottom and George Railings were part of a crowd of nearly three dozen Windy Mountain folk who looked on as the greenies conducted an on-site press conference.

"Have you got proof Tasmanian Tigers live in this orchard?" asked a female television interviewer who had arrived with her producer and cameraman aboard a helicopter that was now parked in a paddock alongside two others.

"Oh yes." Sarah Sarandon straightened her beanie for the cameras. "When we set up camp this morning, three cubs went scurrying from under that tree," she said with a wave of her arm to no tree in particular.

The greenies were in conservationists' heaven. The journalists recorded their every word without question. The only thing not in the greenies' favour was the lack of activity at the orchard. No workmen, no bulldozers, nothing at all was in sight.

As soon as the interview was over, the media contingent — minus Michael Curtis — left en masse in search of Mayor Northan. But they weren't gone long. They couldn't find the Mayor anywhere.

"You just missed another sighting," Sarah taunted the journalists when they arrived back.

"Damn!" said one of the photographers, who was brandishing a camera with a long lens. "What happened?"

"A big Tasmanian Tiger came scurrying across the road," Sarah said. "It had a rabbit squirming in its mouth."

The news crews again left the site, this time in search of a phone box so they could file the first instalments of their stories.

When Birty arrived on his second visit of the day, the gathering had dwindled to the four conservationists, Michael Curtis and the band of curious locals.

"Hey, I want to talk to you people." The sergeant slammed his passenger car door, leaving Stretch behind the wheel, and walked towards the greenies. "Don't think for a moment I don't know what you are up to! I'm not going to stand for any nonsense, you hear?"

Birty veered over to Michael Curtis, who looked up from his novel.

"What's happened to all the other press people?"

"They'll be back." Michael Curtis giggled. "They've gone into town to find a phone box so they can file their copy."

"Do they actually believe this lot?"

"Oh yes, no doubt."

"Like they believed Wish-Wash, eh?" the sergeant said.

"Oh, no," the reporter said. "It's worse this time; much, much worse."

———

MAYOR NORTHAN'S hunch was wrong. As the day progressed, an unlikely alliance was forged in Windy Mountain.

Not many locals had ever had much time for the greenies. Even fewer of them believed in the existence of the Tasmanian Tiger. But sometimes you've got to befriend unfriendly forces in order to defeat a common enemy, and that's what happened. Suddenly, every redneck became a green-neck and every Doubting Thomas became a believer in the Tasmanian Tiger.

Hoo-Chung Loo went to work at his greengrocery wearing a beanie.

Artie Rogerson had been looking forward to a leisurely morning reading the newspapers now he was free of his bikie visitors and had caught up on his sleep. But he didn't get past Page One of *The Pick Of The Crop*. He went in search of a piece of cardboard to write a sign, which he then sticky-taped to the front of the pub's main door. It said in black marking pen, "Down with the Mayor, up with the Tasmanian Tiger. Free cider for conservationists."

Wee Jimmy McMartin rang the Wilderness Society to ask how he could join. The woman at the other end of the line, however, couldn't understand anything he said.

Everywhere Norman J. Hit went he got good feedback about his Page One story. No one had ever patted him on the back before, now everyone was doing it. It began to hurt but mostly in a good way. Then he'd think about what he had written about Moose on Page Three, and cringed.

———————

LOZZA was pegging out washing when she saw Moose approaching across the back paddock. He carried a small knapsack.

"Any luck?" Lozza called.

"No." When Moose stopped next to her she could see he looked ragged, like he had barely slept. "I hauled the new trap to the place I want it. But then I found it was missing a spring in the door."

"Are you going back tonight to fix it?" Lozza pulled the last garment from the washing basket and pegged it.

"Very possibly. If I didn't need to talk to Tiger Kowalski at training this arvo, I'd be going back right away."

Lozza scooped up the empty wicker basket and walked with Moose back towards the house. "Did you put the new trap anywhere near the Mayor's apple orchard?"

"Why would I do that?"

"The greenies next door reckon a family of Tasmanian Tigers are living in Mayor Northan's orchard."

"That's the second time I've heard that in two days!"

"It's in today's newspaper."

"It's what!" Moose's loud reaction frightened two kookaburras, who flapped away from a nearby tree.

Moose followed Lozza inside, where she put down the basket on the kitchen floor, picked the paper up from the table and handed it to him.

Moose sat down and read the Front Page story as Lozza watched his face for a reaction.

Moose started shaking his head. "Why would that reporter even repeat what the greenies had said?"

"Maybe Tasmanian Tigers really do inhabit that orchard?"

Moose tore at his hair. "Come off the grass. Don't you see, the gree-nies are having us on."

"Why would they do that?"

"Every tree is sacred to people like them. But that orchard is next to a busy road. Do you think a creature as shy as the Tasmanian Tiger would go anywhere near it?"

Lozza began opening cupboards, looking for something to cook for lunch as Moose kept staring at the paper. "Don't bother trying to find the article he was writing about you," she said. "I wasted my time walking into town to buy that paper. But I looked at all the sports pages, and zilch."

"Maybe the editor thought it was too boring to run?" Moose said.

"Perhaps it will be in tomorrow?" She put her hands on her hips. "How about an omelette? At least I know we'll have eggs."

Moose nodded, and Lozza disappeared out the back door.

She was gone a long time, which is the only reason Moose perse-vered with the paper. After scanning the sports pages he flipped back to the front and casually turned the page. There, like a beacon, was a photograph of himself staring out of Page Three.

"What the . . . ?" Moose stared at the headlines.

He was still cursing when Lozza returned with two large eggs. She could see he was upset and glanced over his shoulder at the article. She hadn't thought to look in that part of the paper.

———

NORMAN J. HIT was annoyed he hadn't been sent to cover the unravelling story at the orchard. It was his story, after all.

When he arrived at work he was ecstatic that Reg Collins had assigned him that job in the duty book — but then Mr Leggs had wandered out of his office and asked him what he was up to.

"I'm just going now."

"Going where?"

"To James Northan's orchard."

Dobber Leggs eyeballed Reg Collins. "Are you trying to tell me this is a good use of our resources?"

The upshot was the assignment got reassigned. Norman was now walking across the Windy Mountain Football Ground with his wind-sock slung over his shoulder.

He snapped out of his daze when he heard someone call out from the other side of the toilet block. Johnno stood up from where he had been washing brushes under a tap. "Fancy seeing you today. If I were you, I'd be thinking seriously about leaving town before Moose snapped me in half."

"You're joking, right?" Norman felt pale.

"You obviously haven't seen him when he's angry. Anyway, I thought you'd be at the Mayor's orchard following up on your other story today?"

"Nah," Norman said. "My editor has sent our book reviewer instead."

"Are the greenies fair dinkum about their Tasmanian Tiger claims?"

"What do you think! The other day they reckoned the orchard was home to the Green Swift Parrot."

"So you think they're making up the story about the Tasmanian Tiger?"

"I wouldn't put it past them," Norman said. "But if the Mayor has hired who I think he has hired, they don't know what they've got themselves into."

"You think he's hired the bikers from the Applecart?"

"How did you know that?"

"The Big O and I thought the same when we saw them emerge from Mayor Northan's packing shed this morning. We put two and two together."

Johnno squatted back down and turned on the tap. "We're going around there tonight about nine o'clock to see what happens."

Norman looked left and right. "Where is The Big O now?"

"He's gone for a walk." Johnno pulled a face. "He told me cleaning the brushes was easy. You'd think you could trust the word of a priest!"

Then he said, "Why don't you come with us tonight?"

Norman was in two minds. On one hand, he was dying to see what was going to happen at the site. On the other hand, he was suddenly suspicious of the reasons Johnno had come over all matey. "Will, er, um, Moose be going, too?"

"No way. You know how he hates crowds."

———————

"CHRIST, Jimbo, where are you taking us? " Foetus shouted above the engine as the bus rattled up the twisting Jacobs Ladder mountain road.

"We're going up to the snow on Ben Lomond," the Mayor shouted back.

"We don't like snow."

"Why not? it's fun. You can go ski-ing . . . build a snowman— "

The Mayor stopped dead. He felt eyes burning into his head, the closest coming from Foetus who was sitting right next to him in the front seat behind Frizzle, who was driving. Mayor Northan turned sideways. Was it possible the leader of the bikers was getting even bigger? Foetus's voice rose above the roar of the engine and clunking of the gears. "I very much doubt any snow will be up here this late in the season anyway. But that's beside the point. Bikers like us don't ski and we definitely don't build snowmen."

Someone shouted even more loudly from the back of the bus. It sounded like Whish-Willson. "Yeah, can't we go somewhere there's a pub?"

Mayor Northan turned around and forced a smile. "I think you'll find a pub on the top of the mountain."

"Too bad if there is," Foetus said. "As soon as Frizzle finds a place to turn around we're going back down the mountain."

Mayor Northan was vaguely familiar with the democratic process and he didn't object when the bus finally did turn around. But you couldn't fault his determination to keep the group away from Windy Mountain. For the rest of the day, the Mayor tried to take The Muttonbirds to a wildlife park, tourist caves, a hydro lake and even a giant dolls' house.

Foetus got more irritable by the minute. "Jimbo, when are we going back to Windy Mountain? You still haven't told us anything about this job we're doing for you."

Mayor Northan looked at his watch again to check the time. He had managed to keep them away from newsstands and radios all day long. "I suppose I can tell you now. I want you and your gang to pull out the apple trees on my orchard."

"That's a bit beyond our skillset."

"I'm sure it couldn't be that difficult. I've got some saws and some lengths of chain and rope in that toolbox down the back of the bus. I'm sure you'll work it out."

Foetus looked outside to the fading light. "But it'll be dark soon."

"Night is actually the best time to pull out apple trees."

Foetus looked dubious. "Why's that?"

"It's something to do with the apple tree roots," Mayor Northan was glad the former town drunk was down the back where he couldn't hear someone else stealing his tall-tale thunder. "The roots relax at night; they're easier to pull out."

Foetus still didn't look convinced.

Mayor Northan lowered his voice. "Can I level with you, Foetus? Between you and I, some people don't want me to get rid of my orchard. Mostly, they are troublemakers and good-for-nothing greenies."

Foetus snarled. "Oh great! You want us to confront them? didn't you believe me last night when I said we won't break the law for anyone."

"No, you don't understand. This is all perfectly legal. There's not going to be any trouble."

"How can you be sure?"

"That's why we are going in at dark. No one goes near my orchard after dark, even protesters."

"Why not?" Foetus said.

"Well," Mayor Northan said. "The locals say it's haunted."

"Haunted? We can't disturb a spirit."

The Mayor looked around to make sure Whish-Willson wasn't in earshot. "I thought you knew? My orchard is haunted by the ghost of a white man who was responsible for the slaughter of hundreds of your ancestors. He raped your women, kidnapped your children and drove you from your traditional hunting grounds. He desecrated your sacred burial sites and wrote obscene graffiti all over your cave-wall paintings . . . "

Foetus made a fist and shook it. "What was the name of this bastard?"

"John Smith. According to local legend, he roams the orchard at night looking for Aborigines to beat up. You wouldn't be scared of him, would you?"

"Scared? Us?" Foetus had fury in his eyes. "He's the one who should be scared."

Mayor Northan rubbed his hands together. "You know local legend also says John Smith's ghost depends on those apple trees for his energy to remain on this earth. I've even heard it said that whoever destroys the orchard will send the ghost of John Smith to a particularly nasty everlasting after-life."

FOURTEEN
I NEED TO TALK TO YOU, COACH

WHEN MOOSE ENTERED the change shed, he could see only one figure in the dim light.

"I did it!" Tiger Kowalski was coming into focus now. He was sitting on the bench surrounded by all those empty hooks, and he was beaming.

Moose sat down next to him. "What did you do?"

"I got the bet on. You wouldn't believe the odds I got! The fact we haven't actually won a flag in 98 years works very much in our favour. The bookies seem certain we're going to freeze like rabbits in the headli—". He stopped midstream when Moose pulled a pair of boots from his bag and handed them to him. "What are you doing?"

"I'm giving you back Billy Gumboots's proper boots," Moose said. "Wish him luck for me, eh?"

Tiger's smile vanished. "What's going on, cobber?"

"I wanted to explain why I can't play on Saturday."

"What do you mean you can't play? Of course you can play. The umpire dropped the charges."

"You never told me about any parade? I learned about it from a reporter."

"What reporter?"

"That scumbag who wrote the story about me in *The Pick Of The Crop* today."

"I've been too busy to read the paper. But if the parade really worries you, I'm sure we can work something out."

"What would the other blokes think of me if I skipped the parade but still played in the grand final?"

Tiger pinched the bridge of his nose. "You can't do this to me! I've got five thousand dollars riding on this game."

"I'm sorry about that. But I had time to do a lot of thinking last night. I couldn't sleep so I went out hunting all night."

"Didn't I tell you to take it easy? you'll be no good to the team if you need to take a nap in the forward pocket during the grand final."

"You're not listening to me. I'm not going to play."

Tiger buried his head in his hands. When he looked up, he said, "What if I clear it with the other boys?"

"I can't expect them to turn their backs on 98 years of tradition?"

"This club has been in the grand final only five times, so we're only talking about five years of tradition. If push comes to shove, I'm sure the boys would prefer you to be in the team rather than the parade."

"I dunno."

"Do this one thing for me, Moose. Train with us tonight and act like nothing is up. I'll talk to the boys at the end of the session, and sort something out."

———

THE shed came alive with colour and noise as players and support staff arrived in ones and twos.

Pretty soon, clothes were hanging from all but two hooks.

The stink of liniment filled the wooden shed. Head trainer George Lucas was busy in the medical room taping up ankles and strapping thighs. His assistant, Cedric Georges, was applying liniment to the legs of anyone who requested it. Nobody usually took training this seriously. But this was two days before the grand final, the biggest game of most of the players' lives. Outside, a large crowd of supporters had gathered, eager to watch the final training run.

Tiger looked at his watch. He knew whose trousers should be hanging from those two empty hooks. What worried Tiger was Wee Jimmy McMartin and Hoo-Chung Loo were usually the first at training.

Tiger stepped into the centre of the shed. "Gather around boys. I want to say a few things before you go out on to the track."

The footballers formed a noisy circle around the coach. Some stood; others squatted on the concrete floor. Someone called for a little shoosh.

"For some of you this will be the most crucial training night of the year." Tiger shifted his gaze from player to player. "If you take it easy tonight, you might find yourself out of the team. If you train well, you might be a premiership player."

Manny Hjorth asked about arrangements for the parade, which drew moans and groans from the circle of players. Tiger knew not many of them relished that prospect, which is why granting an exemption to Moose was tricky territory.

"Participation in the parade is compulsory," the coach said. "If you're in the team you've got to be in the parade, simple as that."

The players started to groan en masse, but the shed fell silent when Hoo-Chung Loo and Wee Jimmy McMartin walked in.

"Nice of you blokes to turn up," Tiger said. Then he said, "What's with the beanies?"

"We want people to take us seriously," Loo said.

Tiger laughed. "I'd take you more seriously if you were wearing your guernseys and shorts."

"We're not staying for training," Loo said. "We just wanted to tell you something else has come up."

Tiger's jaw dropped. "What?"

"We're going to the protest."

"What protest?"

"Didn't you read today about Northan's orchard? The greenies say they've seen Tasmanian Tigers on the site, but the Mayor has hired some workmen to cut down his trees."

"What on earth has that got to do with you blokes?"

"Apples," Loo said.

"What?" Tiger couldn't believe his ears.

"Apples," Loo said again. "Jimmy needs them for his apple pies and I need them for my green-grocery. If the Mayor destroys his orchard he'll destroy us too."

"Why do your apples need to come from that orchard? Lots of other orchards grow around here."

"We've always got our apples from that orchard. You're too new to this town to understand the importance of the tradition."

The shed became noisy again as the players expressed their mutual outrage.

"Boys," Tiger shouted again. "Can't we keep our minds on the grand final?"

"That's easy for you to say!" Loo said. "The Mayor doesn't want to destroy your business, in fact we all know how he *supports* your business. Our only hope is to get behind the greenies to save the Tasmanian Tiger."

"Aye," spat Wee Jimmy.

"I don't believe this!" Tiger said. "Can't this wait a few days?"

"No, it can't. We're both going to the protest site now."

"For how long?"

"For as long as it takes. All night; all week if we have to. If we miss the grand final, so be it. Football is a hobby. Our livelihood and our families have to come first."

Tiger felt gutted. First, Moose. Now, Loo and Wee Jimmy were seriously thinking about missing the grand final. Loo was the best wingman in the competition and Wee Jimmy was one of the best rovers. The odds he had secured all of a sudden weren't looking that good, after all.

Tiger turned to Moose for help. "You're the Tasmanian Tiger expert here. What do you think about this?"

"If Tasmanian Tigers lived in that orchard, don't you think I'd know about it?"

Loo looked horrified. "The greenies aren't alone. I've seen Tasmanian Tigers there too. So has Jimmy."

Moose shook his head. "Do you blokes really think lying is going to help you?"

Tiger threw up his hands. "This talk is doing us no good at all." He turned to the late arrivals. "I'm begging you Loo, Jimmy, please stay for training, even if you just watch. I'm sure we can work something out. Just give me a little time."

While the other players trained, he called a club committee meeting on the sidelines.

He then called Moose over. 'OK, I've got a deal for you."

"You said you'd talk to the team?"

"And I will. After you've gone.'

————

THEY thought for a moment they had come to the wrong place in the dark. Then they saw someone had cut the chain across the access road, and saw the lights flickering up ahead in the orchard.

Johnno, The Big O and Norman J. Hit walked 30 yards to where the action might be, only to find no action at all. All they saw were the four greenies sitting around a campfire and Peter Salter, who was sitting on a nearby rock

Norman walked over to speak to Salter, who had relieved Michael Curtis. He was armed with a notebook and a pocket camera.

When he returned to the others he was shaking his head. "One of the Windy Mountain policemen was dropping by every hour or so but no one's been around since it got dark. Plenty of onlookers were here — Salty says at one stage there were enough local councillors here to form a quorum — but they disappeared about tea time. He reckons they are probably scared of the ghost."

"I tought lots of media people were supposed to be here?" The Big O said.

"Their deadlines have passed for today."

They sat down on the ground at the side of the access road and waited. Johnno rubbed his hands. It was getting cool and he wished he had worn gloves.

They were nearly ready to give up and go home when they saw oncoming headlights, and scrambled to the other side of the road so they wouldn't get squashed. The greenies linked arms to form a human chain across the road.

As the lights came closer, the sound of grinding gears indicated the driver was slowing down. Then it pulled off the road and parked.

"Hey, I know that truck," Johnno said.

Usually the old flat-tray was laden with fruit and vegetables, and the ever-smiling Hoo-Chung Loo was the sole occupant in the cabin. This time though three figures were silhouetted in the front seat as the truck pulled to a halt.

The first passenger to alight was Wee Jimmy McMartin. From the glow of the truck's headlights, Johnno could see he was wearing a beanie.

Hoo-Chung Loo, the driver, got out next. He was also wearing a beanie.

Then out jumped a giant silhouette.

Few men were that big in Windy Mountain and it took Johnno a few moments to realise who he was seeing.

"Moose?" Johnno said. "I thought you were at training!"

"What are you doing here?"

"I'm here with The Big O and Norman Hit."

"Why are you hanging around with that clot!"

Norman was standing in the shadows. "Hi Moose, I . . . I . . . I . . . I can explain."

"Don't bother. But come anywhere near me, you'd better be wearing a mouthguard."

Loo and Wee Jimmy walked forward to where the greenies were standing across the road.

"We want to join you," Loo said. "We want to save the Tasmanian Tiger too."

"Great," Sarah said. "We don't know how long we must wait though for the vandals to make their move."

Johnno turned to Moose, "Are you joining them too?"

Moose lowered his voice to a whisper. "No way! I'm only here because the coach wants me to keep an eye on Jimmy and Loo. He reckons that my presence might add weight to the greenies' claim and perhaps win a stay of execution for the orchard."

"I got the impression the greenies wanted to save the orchard forever."

"Tiger only needs to save it for a few more days."

Their conversation was interrupted by cries from the protesters. Johnno looked around and saw two blazing headlights turning on to the access road. He felt sure his hunch about the bikers was about to be vindicated.

"It looks like a bus," Sarah said.

"It is." Hoo-Chung Loo watched as the vehicle came into view. "It's Mayor Northan's bus."

The six beanied protesters linked arms. The bus pulled to a halt right in front of them. John Nitram kicked the number-plate.

———

"I THOUGHT you said no one would be here?" Mayor Northan could see the hair inside Foetus's flaring nostrils.

"They're bluffing," the Mayor said. "Drive straight through, Frizzle. I'm sure they'll scatter."

Frizzle put the engine into neutral, pulled on the handbrake, switched on the internal light, rose from the driver's seat and stepped aside. "If you're so sure of that, you drive."

"I . . . I . . . I can't do that."

"Why not?" said Brutus, who was sitting across the aisle near the front of the bus.

"Yeah?" Bluey was sitting next to Brutus.

One of the bikers near the rear of the bus started making chicken noises.

"I . . . I . . . I haven't got a heavy vehicle licence," Mayor Northan said.

"I haven't got a licence to kill." Frizzle breathed his garlic breath down on the mayor. "Who do you think I am? James Bond?"

Wish-Wash was still asleep at the back of the bus, but the bikers and their girlfriends had their eyes fixed to Mayor Northan's head again.

"How was I to know these few greenies wouldn't be afraid of the ghost? But I can only count 10 people out there and I'm sure just the sight of all you bikers will put the wind up them."

No one said a thing, and the Mayor felt compelled to fill the vacuum. As he was saying it, he regretted it.

"I'm offering a bonus for every man who steps off the bus and looks menacing." Did he really just say that? He had already agreed to part with more money than he thought the job was worth.

Foetus looked down at him. "I told you already, we have no intention of breaking the law."

"You don't have to. The mere sight of you will be enough to scare them off."

A voice came from the back of the bus. "Why have we stopped?" Wish-Wash sat up and looked around.

"We're at Jimbo's apple orchard," Foetus said. "He wants us to rip out the trees. Trouble is, a bunch of people outside are trying to stop us from driving further in."

Wish-Wash sprang to his feet and looked straight at Mayor Northan. "You can't destroy this orchard!"

"You keep out of this."

Wish-Wash turned his attention to the bikers. "I thought you liked the cider at The Applecart and the apple pies at Jimmy McMartin's bakery? Where do you think they get their apples from?"

Foetus glared. "You didn't tell us that, Jimbo?"

"Do you want that bonus, or what?" the Mayor snapped. Second thoughts, perhaps the extra outlay would be worth it.

"Well …." Foetus looked around the bus to try to pick up on the general mood.

"I'll tell you what?" the Mayor said, having third thoughts. "Let me talk to them first. Maybe they will move peacefully."

———

THE DOOR hissed open and the Mayor stepped down.

Johnno could see the bikers aboard the bus now, and it looked as if they were having a show of hands. But he couldn't hear what was being said above all the shouting and the trembling of the engine.

The protesters were just silhouettes in the headlights.

"This is private property." The Mayor shielded his eyes and tried to work out who the six people in front of him were. The newspaper had only mentioned four greenies. "You are all trespassing."

"No we're not, man; we're on public land."

"Don't *man* me, sonny," Mayor Northan said. "The driveway you're standing on is not public land. I suggest you leave this property or else."

"Or else what?" That voice came from a female.

"Or else, girlie, I'll have no choice but order that you be removed."

"Haven't you noticed the police aren't here?"

"I don't need police assistance," Mayor Northan said. "I've brought my own men. You have been warned."

"You don't scare us!"

"We'll see about that." Mayor Northan climbed back aboard the bus, where he could be seen waving his hands at a large figure.

When he stepped off, no one followed.

———

"THIS is your last chance," Mayor Northan said. "I can't hold my men back much longer. Move now and no one will get hurt."

"You're wasting your time," shouted the female silhouette. "If you want to get to those apple trees you're going to have to drive right over us."

"Aye," someone said.

"Who said that?" Mayor Northan knew that voice.

"Ach."

"Jimmy McMartin?" Mayor Northan shielded his eyes with his hand. "Is that you? What on earth are you doing here!"

"He's trying to save his livelihood, like me."

"Hoo-Chung Loo?" Mayor Northan said.

"Yes, it is, and I'm not budging."

"I don't know what you're doing here but I'm ordering you to stand aside and let the good men on this bus go about their work."

"And kill all our apples?" Loo said.

"They're not *our* apples," Mayor Northan said. "They're *my* apples. And unless you move, I'll see to it that you never get another one of them again."

"I've got nothing to lose then," Loo said.

"No?" said Mayor Northan. "What about the respect from people in this town? How are you going to live with being branded a filthy, dirty green for the rest of your miserable life in a wheelchair?"

"Is that a threat?"

"No, Loo, it's a promise." Mayor Northan knew he had the full might of The Muttonbirds to back him up. They had voted 13-11 to confront the protesters.

"I'll have to take the risk," Loo said.

"Aye," Wee Jimmy spat.

"OK, if that's the way you want it." Mayor Northan shook his head. He was left with no choice but to fork out the bonuses. He banged on the side of the bus three times because no way was he going to run the garlic gauntlet again. The thing was, only Frizzle had been eating the garlic mountain oysters but his breath alone was enough to keep vampires and Jehovah's Witnesses off the bus.

One by one, the bikers alighted. Johnno gasped. They were armed with saws, rope and chains.

Foetus was first man out, and he roared. "You bludging greenies have got 30 seconds to clear this roadway. We need to sort out that murderous bastard."

Bluey banged his right fist into his left palm over and over. "Yeah. He's had this coming for a long time."

Dilly Brown, who had the headlights shining in her eyes, couldn't see the last speaker's face but she couldn't mistake his voice. In fact, she knew it well.

"Bluey?" she said, breaking the chain so she could shield some of the light from her face with her right hand. "Is that you?"

Bluey couldn't see Dilly properly, either, because it was distorted by the flood of light. But he squinted.

"It's me, your cousin Dilly."

"Dilly?" Bluey said as the two stepped towards each other and embraced. "What are you doing here?"

"I'm trying to save the orchard," Dilly said. "How come you're here?"

"I'm riding with the brothers."

Dilly squealed with delight. She and Bluey, the first born in their respective families, had grown up together. But they had lost touch. The last time they had seen each other was at Bluey's father's funeral. As a young man, he had shunned his heritage.

Bluey turned around. "Hey Foetus! Meet my cuz Dilly."

This was a twist of fate Mayor Northan hadn't banked on. He knew he had to reassert his authority quickly. "This is not a family reunion. Foetus, tell your men that we've got a job to do."

"That's right, guys," Foetus ordered. "We're going to finish what we came here for. Bluey, your cousin Dilly can join us if she likes."

"Join you?" Dilly cried. "Why would I want to join you?"

Wish-Wash had got off the bus last. Now he was standing in the dark trying to work out what was going on as Foetus let fly at Dilly.

"What kind of Aborigine are you, sister?" Foetus bellowed. "How can you stand there and try to prevent us from avenging our fore-fathers?"

"I beg your pardon?" Dilly said.

"All we want to do is punish the ghost of John Smith," Foetus growled.

"John who?" Dilly said.

"John Smith, the murderer and rapist — the white man who drove our people from this land."

"What the hell are you on about?" came a voice from the shadows.

"You keep out of this, Whish-Willson!" the Mayor said.

"I will not." Wish-Wash stepped nearer the light and addressed Foetus. "Who told you the ghost who haunts this orchard is called John Smith?"

"The Mayor did," Foetus said. "Why?"

"He's telling lies," Wish-Wash said.

"You can talk!" Mayor Northan said.

"Shut up, Jimbo," Foetus ordered with a wave of his hand. "Let the man finish."

"The ghost's name is Colonel Richard Northan," Wish-Wash said. "He's the Mayor's great, great, great grandfather and he established this orchard in 1850."

"But he killed Aborigines, right?" Foetus said. "He raped our women and drove us off the land?"

"Not according to the history books," Wish-Wash said. "As far as we know Aborigines never lived in this district. The nearest mob was up in Slutz Plains. It was virgin bush when Colonel Northan came here. He was a tyrant, all right. From all accounts, he treated the convicts under his command with cruelty. He whipped them. He even hanged them. But most of them were Irish."

All eyes turned to Mayor Northan once more.

"You're . . . You're . . . You're not going to believe this fool, are you?" Mayor Northan said. "He's the town drunk!"

"*Ex*-town drunk," shouted The Big O from the roadside.

"Wish-Wash knows his history, man. He used to be a star student."

"Yeah." Sarah stepped forward from the beams of light. "It's not too late for you blokes to join *us*? If the Mayor is allowed to destroy this orchard one of our sacred animals, the Tasmanian Tiger, will be gone forever."

"Don't listen to them," Mayor Northan said. "The Tasmanian Tiger is already extinct."

"No, it isn't," Wish-Wash said. "It's well documented I saw one in the High Street."

"See what I mean about Whish-Willson?" Mayor Northan said. "He tells lies. Tasmanian Tigers do not *exist* any more and there *is* no ghost named Colonel Richard Northan. It's all lies."

"Whoa, hang on," Foetus said. "I don't understand what the Tasmanian Tiger has to do with all this?"

"This orchard is where it lives," Sarah said. "Didn't you read the newspaper this morning?"

"No, we didn't." Foetus spoke slowly as he turned around to Mayor Northan, but the Mayor avoided his gaze. Foetus knew all about body language. Being a parole officer, it was one of the tools of his trade. All of a sudden, everything clicked.

"Now hang on a minute," Mayor Northan said. "I offered you good money to destroy this orchard. I've already advanced you a free day tour and I expect you to carry out your side of the deal."

"You didn't tell us Tasmanian Tigers were living in this orchard?"

"Don't you understand? it's a smokescreen. Not one piece of evidence supports the greenies' claim."

"I've seen Tasmanian Tigers here," Sarah shouted.

"If you don't believe us, hear what Moose has to say." Hoo-Chung

Loo pointed to the big silhouette at the side of the road. "He's a profes-sional Tasmanian Tiger hunter."

Moose was aghast. This was his worst fear come true. It was bad enough he was here. All of a sudden everyone was looking his way.

————

MOOSE didn't want to lie but he didn't want to break the deal he had made with Tiger either.

"Well . . . yes . . . I am looking for the Tiger," he stammered. "I . . . can't . . . really say it's living in this orchard. But I can't rule it out either."

Mayor Northan looked around for support from the bikers. "What would he know?"

"Moose makes his living out of hunting for the Tasmanian Tiger," Hoo-Chung Loo said.

Moose raised an outstretched palm. "Look, I really don't want to get mixed up in this. I've got plenty of other things I'd rather be doing, believe me."

"Like what?" Mayor Northan said. "Injecting yourself with hallu-cinogenic drugs?"

"Moose doesn't take drugs," Loo said.

Mayor Northan shook his head. He knew The Muttonbirds hated drugs as much as they hated alternative life-stylers. "All hippies take drugs. And when they do they see things like pink elephants and Tasmanian Tigers."

"What!" cried Moose.

The Mayor waved his finger. "You're nothing but a drug-crazed troublemaker. Do you really think I'm stupid enough to think these moronic greenies came up with a wild story like this about Tasmanian Tigers on their own?"

"Hang on a minute." Moose felt the blood rushing to his face. "I'm not supporting anyone. I'm here to look after Loo and Jimmy; that's all."

"Why are you telling filthy rotten lies about the Tasmanian Tiger?" Mayor Northan said.

"All I said was I can't rule out the possibility Tasmanian Tigers come to this orchard."

"Why don't you tell the truth?"

"I don't *know* the truth about the Tasmanian Tiger," Moose said. "If I knew exactly where the Thylacine lived I would have caught one by now. The Tasmanian Tiger might well live in this orchard. It might bloody-well like eating apples."

"Hey," Bluey said. "He might have hit on something. When Wish-Wash saw a Tasmanian Tiger walking down the main street he said it smelt like it had been eating apples."

Mayor Northan was beside himself. "He's the town drunk, for God's sake!"

"*Ex*-town drunk," The Big O said again. "God replaced him."

"Can't you shut up, you Irish twit! Whatever he is, it doesn't matter! The Tasmanian Tiger ate meat, not apples. *Past* tense!"

"Is that so, Mr Expert?" Moose had had about as much as he could stomach.

Moose walked closer to Foetus. "Do you blokes want to help me out here?"

"What did you have in mind?"

"Get me some strong rope," Moose said.

Mayor Northan backed up a step but only into the grasp of Brutus and Frizzle. He looked left and right, and got another blast of garlic. "What do you think you are doing?"

"A little experiment," Moose took the rope Bluey had coiled over one shoulder.

"Unhand me! I'm warning you!" Mayor Northan tried to wriggle free.

"March him to that gum tree." Moose pointed to the edge of the orchard.

"What . . . what . . . what do you think you are up to?" With the help of two more bikers, Brutus and Frizzle dragged the Mayor kicking and screaming into the orchard. The mob followed with their flashlights.

Mayor Northan was pushed down on to his knees, back to the tree. He burst into tears when he thought he saw Moose eying off an overhanging branch.

"Please don't do this," he pleaded. "I've got a family. Please don't hang me."

"Be a man, we're not going to hang you."

"You're not?" Mayor Northan sobbed. "What . . . what . . . what is the rope for then?"

"I told you, I'm just doing a little experiment."

"An experiment?" Mayor Northan whimpered. "You're going to whip me, aren't you?"

"Sheesh. You could have waited until we were gone to relieve yourself!" Moose shook his head. "I was never going to whip you. I've got a much more interesting experiment in mind."

"What?"

"I want to see if the Tasmanian Tiger prefers meat or apples, so I'm going to tie you to the tree and leave you here overnight."

"You can't leave me here! Everyone knows the orchard is haunted. What about the wild beasts!"

"I don't think your great, great, great grandfather would hurt you, would he? And you don't even believe in Tasmanian Tigers, do you?" Moose tied the Mayor's hands behind his back then looped the rope around the tree and Mayor Northan several times and tied it tightly.

A flash of light snapped as Peter Salter took a photograph. Moose stepped back to admire his rope-work. "I hope that wet patch on your trousers doesn't show up in print."

"You can't do this!" Mayor Northan shouted, as he watched everyone walk away laughing into the darkness, leaving him only a fading *hee-haw, hee-haw* sound.

FIFTEEN
LOCK HIM UP!

BIRTY AND CONSTABLE SMITH went to Blackstump Road at 4am to arrest Moose.

A bleary-eyed Johnno answered the door. "What are you going to charge him with?" Johnno said angrily as they handcuffed their prisoner. "Tying a mayor to an apple tree between the hours of sunset and sunrise?"

Moose was charged with assault and unlawful imprisonment, and he didn't deny it.

Mayor Northan had been tied to that tree for more than three hours. After everyone else had left, Salter had the cheek to return and ask for an official comment.

"Release me . . . get help," Mayor Northan had groaned.

"I can't do that. It's my job to report the news, not be a part of it. Besides, I've got a deadline to meet."

So Mayor Northan was left alone in the dark. He tried calling out for help but he couldn't be heard as far away as town. And no good Samaritans walked by. Who would? Everyone knew the ghost of Colonel Richard Northan roamed the orchard at night.

The Mayor was finally rescued when Constable Smith, guilty he hadn't checked on the protesters all night because he, too, was scared of the ghost, finally plucked up the courage to drive to the site. When he arrived, there were no lights, no greenies, no media, no spectators, nothing. He nervously rolled down his window to listen for any tell-tale sounds as he drove the police car slowly up the access road.

That's when he heard a faint groan.

Constable Smith stopped, cut the engine, and listened.

"Help me, help me," the voice said. "Over here."

"Who . . . who . . . who are you?" the terrified Constable Smith called out.

"I'm the Mayor, you idiot. Help me. NOW."

After he was released, the Mayor insisted Smithy awaken Sergeant Birtwistle.

"I want a Royal Commission into this. Arrest them; arrest the lot of them."

Birty managed to calm the Mayor down enough to rule out most of the arrests he demanded. He said freedom of the Press deterred him from arresting Peter Salter. It wouldn't be good politics to arrest the local greengrocer nor the baker. If he arrested the greenies they would become martyrs, and no one, especially Mayor Northan, wanted that to happen, did they? The Big O, Norman J. Hit and Les Johnson had been innocent bystanders. And Windy Mountain jail lacked the facilities to house large numbers of bikers.

"Get Moose Routley then." Mayor Northan was sipping hot cocoa while wrapped in a blanket at the police station. "If you had arrested those bikers when they arrived in town, like I asked, none of this would ever have happened."

Birty bit his tongue. If the Mayor had been looking at him, he might have detected a bit of an eye roll.

———

"WHY DID he do it?" Dobber Leggs shouted as he waved his soggy newspaper with the photograph of the Mayor tied to the tree.

"It explains why in the story," Reg Collins said. "It was a test to see whether the Tasmanian Tiger preferred to eat apples or meat."

"Not that, you fool! I'm talking about Sean McWhirter. Bad enough Peter Salter even took the photo, but why would any responsible person run it on Page One? I didn't even know we could run photos that big?"

"Would you have preferred it was tucked inside the paper?" Reg Collins said. The editor seemed to be sitting on a bubbling spa jet. Either that or he was making the water around him boil.

"If you had fired McWhirter in the first place we would have none of this trouble." Dobber Leggs splashed his left fist down on to the water again.

It was shortly after 8.30am.

The headlines on the front of *The Pick Of The Crop* had never been bigger nor bolder,

MAYOR TIED TO TREE

The story was accompanied by a photograph that showed the Mayor lashed to the tree, with both his face and trousers worse for wear.

"That will teach him to mess with the Tasmanian Tiger," Sarah Sarandon was quoted as saying.

The editor continued to bubble. "Mayor Northan was on the phone at half-past-five this morning. I tried to stop the print run but it was too late. Then I tried to get the copies pulped, but that was too late too. They were already hitting people's lawns."

The conversation was interrupted when Tiger Kowalski appeared through the door. He looked awful. "I heard Moose has been arrested!"

"He's in the lock-up now," Collins said.

Tiger tugged at his hair. "It's all my fault. Any chance he'll get out on bail in time to play in the grand final?"

"I dunno. It's a pretty serious charge."

When Tiger left, the editor turned to the chief-of-staff again. "That reminds me, Reginald," he said. "Any further progress on the cow presentation?"

Collins shook his head. "I've tried everything I could think of to get permission to hold the draw on the ground. Yesterday I even tried Tiger to see if he could use his influence with the Mayor."

"And?"

"And he said he didn't think he'd have any luck, but he'd see what he could do. I haven't had a chance to talk to him since."

"He was just here!" The editor pointed to the door as he spoke shrilly. "Why on earth didn't you ask him about it?"

"I think our cow would be about the last thing on his mind, don't you? I think we will just have to accept just outside the boundary line is the nearest we're getting."

Dobber Leggs's pupils circumnavigated his eye sockets.

"Look, it's not my fault. I've tried everything I could."

"You obviously haven't tried hard enough. I ask you to do one little thing . . ."

"OK . . . I'll have another go." Collins hung his head, mainly to hide the face he was pulling.

"Let's move on, shall we? What have you got planned today in the way of news, Reginald?"

The chief-of-staff lifted his head. "I've got two reporters and three photographers rostered on to cover the parade tonight. I wouldn't think Moose has a hope in hell of getting out of jail, but if he does I can't wait to see what kind of reception the Mayor gets when he presents him to the crowd. What are the chances of them even shaking hands?"

"I think we'll need to supervise McWhirter tonight. We need to ensure he runs the photo of our cow on Page One."

"Won't you want a photo from the actual presentation on the front?"

The penny dropped for the editor when he looked the chief-of-staff in the eye. "I don't believe it! Don't tell me you haven't organised for the cow to be in the grand final parade either?"

———

NORMAN J. HIT was walking to work when a camper van pulled in next to him. The window was wound down by a man who leant over from the driver's seat. He wore a loud checked suit, a large hat and a little bow tie.

"Is this where the bushrangers are at?" He spoke in a cowboy drawl.

"Pardon?"

"The bushrangers? You know? Ned Kelly and his gang?"

"Ned Kelly was never from around here. Besides, he's dead."

"Dead? How did he die?"

"He was hanged."

"Oh boy! I didn't know you crazy Aussies still hanged bushrangers. I'd love to get a video of that thang to take back to the States."

The visitor was sixtyish.

"Is this town called Windy Mountain, son?" The American scratched the stubble on his chin as he surveyed the High Street through the front window.

"Yes. Where is it you want to go?"

"Looks like I'm already here."

Before Norman knew it, the American was standing on the footpath. He held out his hand. "Howdy, my name is Tim Noah Junior." When he smiled, his teeth were whiter than his big hat, and showed off his gold tooth.

Norman Hit cautiously shook hands and introduced himself. "I'm a reporter with the local newspaper."

"A goddam RE-porter? Here? Well, I'll be damned." Tim Noah slapped his right thigh. "It doesn't seem to matter where I go. What is it you want to ask me?"

"Pardon?"

"You're a RE-porter. Ask me some questions."

"What about? I don't even know who you are."

The Texan looked puzzled. "You must have heard of me?"

"You're the one who stopped to talk to me."

Tim Noah looked down the main street of Windy Mountain again.

"Mighty perty little town you have here. I imagined the OUT-back would be different though. Ya'll in the middle of a carnival?"

Norman shook his head. "We've tarted up the town in support of our football team that is playing off in the grand final tomorrow."

Noah frowned.

"Are you looking for anyone in particular, Mr Noah?"

"Matter of fact, son, I am. I'm paying a SUR-prise visit on a guy by the name of Moose Routley. Can you point me in his DIR-ection?"

"Ah," Norman said. He pointed to the police station across the road. "See that building over there . . ."

————

"HOWDY, sheriff." Tim Noah offered his hand. "They tell me you've got one of my men in your jail."

"One of *your* men?"

"I'm Tim Noah from Dallas, Texas. Moose Routley is on my payroll.
"

Birty eyed Noah suspiciously. "You sure you're not another mainland reporter trying to con his way into seeing Moose for an exclusive interview? I've had a gut-full of you people today."

"Shoot, do I look like a RE-porter?" Noah pulled a wad of notes from his coat pocket and started thumbing through them. "I'm here to post his bail. How much do you need?"

Birty shook his head. "In this country bail can only be granted by a magistrate. Moose will have to be our guest until the court convenes on Monday."

"But I go back home on Sunday!"

Birty scratched his scalp. "What did you say he does for you exactly?"

"He's looking for the TAS-manian Tiger for me. Plus, he helps me out with Tasmanian souvenirs . . . bushranger stuff mainly."

Birty smiled. "We don't have a lot of bushrangers any more."

"How many have you hanged already?"

"What?"

"The world would never forgive you if you drove the bushrangers into EX-tinction too? Or are they just hiding deep in the bush like the TAS-manian Tigers?"

"What?"

"You sure you won't take this money?" Noah looked down at the coloured notes in his hand. "Can't say I blame you. It doesn't look real to me."

Birty exhaled. "Best I can do is let you see Moose for five minutes. Follow me."

He walked down the hallway and unlocked a heavy steel door that led to the cell. "Make it quick."

Moose was surprised to see the American and knew he had to do some fancy footwork explaining what had happened.

As he talked, though, he twigged he was actually rising in Noah's estimation with every word.

"Ain't no one ever thought of tying mayors to trees back home," Noah said. "I haven't figured out how yet, but something tells me I can use this to my AD-vantage."

That's all the encouragement Moose needed to keep spinning his yarn.

"I've been tracking the Tiger in that apple orchard for 18 months," he lied. "Now the Mayor wants to destroy its habitat. He deserved what was coming to him."

———

MAYOR Northan was sipping camomile tea when the door burst open.

The fright caused him to knock the mug over his finely polished desk.

"Have you ever heard of knocking?" he said when he saw it was Tiger Kowalski. In his haste to mop up the mess with tissues he ripped from a box, he didn't notice Tiger's nostrils were flaring. "I've

told you before, we shouldn't meet here. If anyone sees us together—
"

"Do you think I really care about that now? My best footballer is in jail because of you."

"Keep your voice down." By now the Mayor had three yellow-soaked mounds in front of him but he had stopped the lava flows. "I feel sorry for you, of course, but I have to tell you, as far as I'm concerned, Moose Routley can rot in jail."

"Birty tells me I can forget about him getting out in time for the grand final!"

The Mayor shrugged. "Nothing I can do to prevent the law taking its course."

"You could drop the charges."

"After what he did to me?" The Mayor jumped to his feet. "I want you to leave my office *now*."

Tiger shook his head. "I'm not going anywhere, you corrupt fuckwit."

"You can't talk to me like that . . . have some respect. I'm the Mayor. I've got a good mind to call the police."

Tiger shoved the black phone on his desk towards him. "Be my guest. I'm sure Birty will be very interested in what I have to say about you. you'll probably have to share a cell with Moose."

"I beg your pardon?"

"I think the Taxation Department might be very interested too."

"Shoosh." The Mayor gestured with his hands. "Someone might hear." He glanced out the window to the High Street. "Anyway, I've done nothing illegal."

"How long has it been legal to run a brothel in Tasmania?"

The Mayor relaxed and smiled. "I've certainly never had anything to do with red-light establishments."

"Ask just about anyone in this town how the Dancing School really makes its money. Some members of the Masonic Lodge are regular clients. Aren't you the Grand Poohead? Why don't you ask them?"

"This is a trick." The Mayor's eyes widened.

"It's no trick. I've got documents with your signature on. I've got lists of clients, too, which include some very respectable names with some very interesting interests. It's all documented. I'll bring you and half of this damn town down unless you drop those charges."

"You're bluffing. You can't tie me to any of that?"

"Oh, can't I? Who owns the building? You do. Who pays the girls? You do. The documents prove it. I might even run off some copies for the media too. I hear a few of them are around town."

Mayor Northan put his hands on his temples. "This is . . . this is blackmail."

"You can interpret it any way you like."

"Don't be a fool. If you went to the police, you'd bring yourself down too."

"I don't care," Tiger said. "I'm prepared to go to any lengths to get that premiership. Besides, I haven't got as much to lose as you. And I know I can handle jail. You though? Hmm! Good luck sharing the cell with Moose, for starters."

Tiger turned to leave.

"OK, wait." Mayor Northan headed Tiger off at the door and stood in front of him to block his exit. "I'll have the charges dropped."

"When?"

"Today! This afternoon! As soon as I can!"

"Take all the time you need. But if Moose isn't out of jail by 3pm, I'm going to the police." He pushed the Mayor out of the way, placed his hand on the doorknob and turned around. "Don't feel too bad about all this. Remember, it's your football team as much as mine. Our Dancing School is chief sponsor."

Mayor Northan walked back across the room and slumped into his chair.

He was drying his sweaty forehead and hands with a handkerchief when someone knocked.

"Come in." Mayor Northan's whole body had gone numb.

"Howdy, Mr Mayor," said the man in the 10-gallon hat who entered. "I'm Moose Routley's BENE-factor."

Mayor Northan leapt up before Noah even had the chance to close the door. "You can kindly leave then. I don't know how you got past my secretary without an appointment."

"*She* was happy to take my money." Instead of leaving, Noah sat down on the other side of the desk. "I think you ought to hear me out, sir. My proposal might be LUC-rative to you."

The Mayor resumed his seat. "Lucrative?"

The intruder seemed to be staring at the yellow mounds of tissues in front of him as if he was wondering what to make of them.

"I had an accident."

"I heard about that. I haven't seen the newspaper yet but I hear it was perty obvious from the PHOTO-graph."

"Look, if you came here to ridicule me, I really think you should leave before I call security."

"I think you'll find the fat man in the uniform who was sitting at the front door has gone to the shop to buy an EX-pensive ice-cream." Noah belly laughed. "He came into some money too."

The American stopped laughing. "The good news for you is I've still got plenty left where that money came from. The only question is how much are you going to charge me to buy your orchard?"

"You want to buy it?"

"If we can come to terms, yessir. That oughtn't be too hard. They tell me you've been trying to sell that land for years."

"What if I have been?"

"It tells me you must be perty keen to OFF-load it."

"And what would you do with it?"

"My man tells me TAS-manian Tigers are living on that land. I not only want to preserve it as a wildlife park, I want to build a theme park on the edge of the site. I figure it will attract TOUR-ists from all over the world."

"You're kidding me?"

"Imagine the money I'd make from the tours? What kid wouldn't want to go on the TAS-manian Tiger ride? And I'm sure people would pay good money to get their photos in front of that big ol' tree where the bushranger Moose Routley once tied up the Mayor in order to save that big cat. I reckon I'd make me another million dollars."

A million dollars? The Mayor's eyes lit up with dollar signs as the life returned to his shell-shocked body.

"I'm afraid the orchard is not for sale."

"Not for sale? What are you talking about?"

"My plans for the orchard have changed. I want to set up a wildlife park of my own, leave the apples right where the Tigers can get them. And I'm going to have that gum tree removed to make room for *my* theme park."

———

"DID YOU hear?" Norman J. Hit said. "They let Moose out of jail. Mayor Northan decided to drop the charges."

Johnno and The Big O had been sitting on the grass drinking mugs of tea for smoko break when Norman arrived.

"He dropped the charges?" Johnno's eyes widened. "Like that umpire dropped the charges?"

"I had the same thought at first. But the Mayor said he did it so Moose would be free to play in the grand final. He said he felt it was his civic duty."

The Big O nearly choked on the biscuit he had dunked. "Since when did dat Mayor become so big-hearted!"

"Perhaps a few hours alone in that orchard changed him for the better?" Norman said.

"You tink?" The Big O stared at him in disbelief.

Norman shrugged. "Is Oodles around?"

"He was here five minutes ago when he opened up the shed so we could get some hot water from the urn," Johnno said. "Where's Moose now?"

Norman threw back his shoulders again. "I think he's gone into hiding. All the journos in town want to interview him. Sergeant Birtwistle wouldn't let them speak to him while he was in jail so they set themselves up outside the front door. My guess is he left out the back and is hiding at the Dancing School. Good luck him avoiding the bloodhounds when he's in the parade tonight though."

———

TOWNSFOLK lined the High Street around dusk for the grand final parade.

Fathers hoisted their knee-high children on to their shoulders, and older kids scaled poles and balconies to catch a glimpse of their heroes.

Mainland media people jostled each other for the best vantage points too.

Tim Noah felt sure the journalists were actually looking for him. He tried to disguise himself by taking off his hat.

The local cub troop marched into sight first. Akela Squirrel Squires led fifteen of them down the High Street, heads high and arms swinging.

The cubs were followed by the marching girls.

"They sure are perty!" Tim Noah shouted, forgetting for a moment he was trying to be inconspicuous.

"Who's that loud-mouth yank?" Councillor Spot Billings asked Oodles.

"I've never seen him before. He must be one of the media people. *American Sixty Minutes* perhaps?"

The Windy Mountain Brass Band came next. They consisted of about two dozen men and women dressed in maroon uniforms with brass buttons. A thick-set man carrying a brass drum kept the beat while the others blasted away on an assortment of trumpets, trombones and even a sousaphone.

Three men with beards and leather jackets followed the band. They were leading a cow on a rope. One of the men was carrying a shovel and a bucket.

Dobber Leggs couldn't believe his eyes.

"Is that our cow, Reginald? Those men with her look like bikers to me."

"This must be down to Norman J. Hit."

"For goodness sake, who gave Norman Hit permission to hire The Muttonbirds to lead our cow?"

Reg Collins shook his head. "I told Norman to try Oodles one more time. They must have worked something out."

Dobber Leggs's bellow could be heard even above the noise of the parade. "If anything happens to that cow I will hold you personally responsible."

The Windy Mountain football team came next. The players rode on the trays of five utes that slowly carried them down the main street. Tiger Kowalski waved to the crowd. The players were wearing their guernseys and numbers, and waved, too — though it was fairly obvious they didn't really want to be anywhere near the hoopla.

"Which one is Moose Routley?" one of the mainland journalists asked Hilda Hinchcliffe.

"I'm not sure," Mrs Hinchcliffe said.

"That's him!" Artie Rogerson cried. "Number one, see."

"No, it's not," Betty Jacobson said. "That's Brian Billson, who's now captain of the reserves."

The utes pulled into a roped-off area and the spectators converged around them. The footballers made their way through the throng, into the front door of the Dancing School and then emerged upstairs on the balcony where Mayor Northan was waiting with a microphone ready to introduce the players.

The crowd started a chant. "We want Moose, we want Moose."

Tiger grabbed the microphone from the Mayor and called for calm. "I have some bad news. Moose has had to pull out of the team."

A hush came over the crowd.

"It's a trick!" shouted Reverend George Beare, a lone voice in a sea of stunned silence.

Tiger shook his head. "The truth is, Moose is suffering from post-jail depression. He's in no condition to play in the grand final. We will have to win it without him."

————

MOOSE sat watching the ceremony from the hospital balcony alongside Foetus whose leg was elevated on a stool.

They listened as Tiger announced Moose's withdrawal from the team.

Foetus turned to him and squinted. "Post-jail depression? I didn't think you looked that bad."

Moose smiled and shook his head. "I did another deal with Tiger. It's part of our tactics."

"What are you talking about?"

"It's a ploy to keep the Saints guessing. Tomorrow, we'll have 20 players run on to the ground and I won't be among them. But just before the siren, I'll run on to the ground and someone will run off."

"Bet your life all those mainland journos have staked out the farmhouse."

"Tiger has thought of that. I'm going to stay with him tonight."

SIXTEEN
BULLSHIT, BULLSHIT ... WE WANT THE FOOTY

A CHILLY WIND blew towards the southern goals on grand final day. Locals judged it to be worth at least three goals to the team kicking that way.

Most of Windy Mountain's citizens — nearly all 3003 or 3004 of them — had turned out for the biggest football match of the year. They had been joined by about the same number of people who were backing the Slutz Plains Saints. The ground was a sea of yellow and black, and red, white and black scarves, beanies, gloves and guernseys.

The Windy Mountain Brass Band struck up a tune in the middle of the oval.

"Bullshit, bullshit . . . we want the footy," the crowd chanted.

———

BIRTY had arrived at the game early, thinking he'd have time for a meat pie while he was soaking up the atmosphere before his last-ever shift.

But when he caught sight of Johnno, he nearly choked.

"I don't believe this." He sprayed bits of meat, sauce and spit as he spluttered. "Look, over there, Stretch. He's wearing a dress again, and this time in broad daylight."

"So he is." Junior Constable Stretch looked to where Johnno was sitting in a fold-up chair drinking a stubby. He was wearing a yellow and black dress.

"Now we're going to have to arrest him again and miss some of the match."

"On what charge, sarge? He's not the only one drinking in public."

"Yes, but he's the only man dressed in blinking women's clothing."

"That's not against the law, sarge."

"How can the blinking law have changed in a week?"

"It hasn't. The law says men are prohibited from wearing women's clothes *between the hours of sunset and sunrise*. It says nothing about *between the hours of sunrise and sunset*."

"Unbelievable! We'll have to wait until it gets dark to nick him then."

"I doubt he's going to let that happen," Stretch said. "Look at him. He's trying to rile you. "

Sure enough, Johnno was looking at the two coppers now and he had a big grin on his face.

"Don't let him get to you, sarge. Ignore him. Enjoy the game."

Birty exhaled deeply and tried to focus back on the game about to begin.

"Look at those patches of mud," he said. "I hope the boys are wearing their long stops."

The crowd cheered as the Windy Mountain players crashed through a banner.

"There's Smithy," Stretch said. "But Tiger wasn't lying about Moose Routley. I can't see him out there."

Birty looked smug. "It's an old ploy, son. I bet Moose runs on to the ground just before the siren."

But he was wrong.

When the Slutz Plains captain won the toss and elected to kick with the assistance of the wind, the players took up their positions. Hoo-

Chung Loo went to his wing, Wee Jimmy McMartin started in the forward pocket, Spiros Firos headed to centre half-forward, Manny Hjorth went to the centre, Billy Gumboots went to the half-forward flank, and Brian Billson and Colin Feeney ran to the bench.

————

MOOSE was back at the Windy Mountain Hospital, this time as a patient. He had woken up all jaundiced and weak. When Tiger took him to the hospital he was diagnosed as having hepatitis, probably the same strain as Foetus's.

In the absence of an isolation ward, it made sense for them to share the same room.

Bubby Throsby had finally gone home, but he had left a note in the drawer of the bedside table, which Moose opened to store his wallet and keys.

The note said —

To whom it may concern:

So very sorry you have to share the room with this obnoxious bikie but believe me he was much worse the day he came in.

I had to take matters into my own hands to make him settle down. Best $50 I ever spent paying for my mate Bob to shave his pubes. Foetus has been much more subdued since.

The thing is he thinks Sister Daisy Rowbottom put Bob up to it. If you know what's good for you, you won't tell him it was really me. It would only make him angry again.

————

TIGER Kowalski had put on a brave face in his pre-match address. "Let's win this premiership for Moose."

"Does that mean I get my footy boots back?" Billy Gumboots said.

Tiger shook his head. "It all happened so quickly. He did give me the boots back but I can't remember where I put them down."

Slutz Plains had two goals on the board before Windy Mountain posted its first score, a point.

The Saints' bigger ruckmen were winning the tap and getting the ball moving quickly towards the wind-assisted goals.

The Tigers were well served, however, by Billy Gumboots, who relished being back on the big stage. He touched the ball a number of times and was very steady on his feet when others went sliding in the mud. But every time he tried to kick the football, one of his rubber boots flew off.

At quarter-time, the visitors led 4.5 (29) to 1.1 (7).

"Isn't this SOME-thing!" Tim Noah said to Mitch Mitchell, *The Pick Of The Crop's* copyboy, who was standing next to him in front of the pie stand.

Billy copped an earful from Tiger in the quarter-time huddle. "For Christsakes, don't try to kick the ball, Billy; handball it to someone else. Every time you have to retrieve your gumboot and put it back on, the team is one man down for at least 30 seconds."

Windy Mountain hit back in the second quarter with the help of the wind. Billy's handballs brought some of his teammates into the game. Tiger had also made some telling positional changes. Hoo-Chung Loo was moved into the centre where he sharked the ball repeatedly. The Flying Dutchman went to full-forward, and Wee Jimmy McMartin started on the ball.

The Saints were kept scoreless against a strengthening wind and the half-time score was Windy Mountain 6.4 (40) to Slutz Plains' 4.5 (29).

———

AFTER the teams disappeared into their sheds at half-time, the crowd was entertained by the Windy Mountain Brass Band, this time with a trombone solo in B Flat by Terry Mason.

"And now it's time to announce the winner of *The Pick Of The Crop's* name-the-cow competition," a voice over the public address system said as Norman J. Hit led the cow on a rope to the half-forward flank. He wasn't alone. Three clean-shaven giants walked with him. Bringing up the rear was Dobber Leggs, who seemed very surprised to be there with Mitch Mitchell, who was rolling a small barrel from which the winning entry was to be drawn.

Norman felt very proud of himself for enlisting the support of The Muttonbirds. He felt sure he'd be rewarded for his initiative. But it was win-win. He also felt sure Brutus, Frizzle and Bluey appreciated the business transaction he had put to them, not to mention their glowing pride the US would soon know about their bushranger infamy.

Mayor Northan was aghast.

"Get that cow off the ground immediately," he bellowed at Oodles, who was standing on the sidelines next to him.

"Not me," Oodles said. "I've got no intention of being tied to a goalpost."

"But you have to do what I say."

"Tell them that." Oodles pointed to the rest of the bikers who had gathered outside the fence near the forward pocket.

The draw went ahead unhindered. The winner's name was Gus Foot, who wasn't at the ground but had correctly guessed the cow's name was Daisy.

———

THE Saints had the wind again in the third quarter, and it was stronger than it had been all day. The visitors reeled off five goals. Windy Mountain did score one lucky goal near the end of the quarter but trailed 7.4 (46) to 9.5 (59) at the final break.

"Come on you blokes," Tiger pleaded in the huddle. "Thirteen points down is *nothing* in this wind. We've got the breeze behind us."

The Tigers, however, didn't count on the vagaries of the wind. One minute it was blowing strongly, the next it stopped dead. Where it went, no one knew.

Through sheer effort, however, Windy Mountain wore the Saints' defence down. The Tigers scored their first goal at the seven-minute mark and their second goal 15 minutes later. The margin was now one point in the Saints' favour.

For the next five minutes, the ball sea-sawed from end to end. The players became embroiled in an all-in brawl near the centre. Spiros Firos was knocked unconscious and had to be removed from the ground on a stretcher.

Tiger moved Billy Gumboots into the centre, Hoo-Chung Loo from the centre to the half-forward flank and brought 20th man Brian Billson from the bench to centre half-forward.

With 41 seconds to go, Loo trapped the ball near the boundary line, scooped it up and landed a short stab pass on Wee Jimmy McMartin's chest 75 yards out from goal. As the Scotsman marked, Brian Billson ran past on his inside calling for the handpass. "I'm clear, I'm clear," he yelled.

Jimmy went with what he thought was a safer option. It was no secret Billson couldn't kick very well, which is why he had lost the captaincy. Jimmy baulked around two Saints, bounced the ball and handpassed over an opponent's head into the arms of Smithy who was unmarked.

But as Smithy turned, he pivoted on a cow pat, slipped and the ball tumbled to the ground.

The siren was going to blow any moment.

With the Saints clinging on by one point, a desperate race for the ball ensued.

A Slutz Plains' defender was first on the scene, a step or two in front of Billy Gumboots, and everyone knew all he had to do was dive on the ball and bottle up play until the siren.

But he, too, slipped on the same cowpat.

Sure-footed Billy scooped up the ball and looked up. No one stood between him and the goals.

"Kick it, kick the fucking thing," a teammate cried.

It seemed to happen in slow motion.

Both the blue gumboot and the ball left Billy's foot at the same time. The boot tumbled 10 yards in a blue blur and the ball kept on wobbling toward the big sticks.

The ball cartwheeled end over end.

Just when it looked like it was going to fall at least five yards short, a gust of wind inexplicably kicked up and carried it a further four yards.

The siren blew, which meant the Tigers were one lousy yard short of the premiership!

AFTERWORD

THE 1935 LAW banning men from wearing female apparel in public between sunset and sunrise was repealed in the Tasmanian parliament in November 2000.

Johnno left Windy Mountain shortly after the grand final.

But he returns 28 years later in a very different role.

Find out what nonsense unfolds in the next book in the Windy Mountain series.

28 YEARS LATER

BOOK 7 OF THE WINDY MOUNTAIN SERIES

When someone threatens to spoil Christmas by demolishing Windy Mountain's historic cafe, it's time to take sides.

The proposed replacement is an ugly commercial building that would tower over the sleepy town.

The quirkiness of this funny series goes to a new level when a Tiger Shark surfaces. Tasmanian Tigers make their customary appearance too.

EXCERPT FROM CHAPTER 1

BOX OF TRICKS

THE OLD MAN in the suit kept yabbering as he unlocked P.O. Box 15. "Did Clarence look sick to you the last time you saw him?"

When he stepped back with two letters in his hand, Wendy was looking daggers at him.

"Is something wrong?" James Northan said.

"How long have you had that post office box, love?"

"Not long. Why do you ask?"

"I've had my name down for a higher-up one for two years! Bending down to the bottom row every day does my back in."

"What can I say?" James pretended to adjust one of his hearing aids, but it was only to give himself time to come up with a plausible explanation. "The local postmaster has got it into his head I am somehow behind the new development. He is wrong, of course. But if people want to try to curry favour, who am I to stop them?"

Wendy frowned. "What new development?"

"You really do not know?" James twiddled his other hearing aid. "I thought you would have been advised by now!"

————

Wendy was not used to seeing anyone else on the post office verandah at this hour — just before dawn, before the heat of the day.

A yellow glow came from the fluorescent strip bolted to the red-brick outer wall of the building, but the only other light came from a flashing red and green reindeer in the window of her cafe next door.

She had been rummaging around in her handbag looking for the key when she heard approaching footsteps on the concrete path and looked in that direction.

She had never been so relieved to see the former mayor come around the corner dressed in his familiar suit, shiny, black shoes and old school tie, and carrying a briefcase, as if he were going to chambers.

James recoiled and clutched his chest. "You scared me half to death, Wendy!"

"Nice to see you, too, love," she shrieked, reaching a higher pitch than her normal gravelly voice that had been deepened by thirty-five years of smoking.

She didn't even know James was renting one of the 45 private boxes. Why would he? The letterbox at his gate was more elaborate than some houses in this town.

She had last seen him on his 83rd birthday.

He had been sharing a three-bedroom, one-bathroom weatherboard house with two other old men, Clarence 'Oodles' Noodle, 85, and Bert 'Wish-Wash' Whish-Willson, 84, for three months of quarantine.

Friends and relatives wanted to keep the three elderly men out of reach of COVID-19.

But James hated being locked up with lesser beings. Oodles had once worked for him at the council and was still wearing the same overalls, Bert had once been the town drunk who, in James's mind, had brought disgrace on the town by claiming to have seen a Tasmanian Tiger, the problem being the species had been listed by the Government as extinct.

Wendy had tried to cheer James up on his birthday by taking him a strawberry cheesecake and setting it up with candles on a table in the front yard.

But it didn't seem to make him any happier.

James studied her for a moment, like he was trying to work out a clue for one of his beloved cryptic crosswords. "Your hair looks quite drab in this light, Wendy."

Really? How rude!

Her grey hair had nothing to do with the flashing light. Something had to give as money got harder to come by. She had a packet-a-day cigarette habit, and the comfort of a nicotine hit rated higher right now than her monthly trips to the hairdresser for blonde tints.

He'd find out in time her hair really was 'drab' these days.

Instead of dignifying his comment with an explanation, she asked him a question.

"How come I haven't seen you or Oodles and Wish-Wash at the cafe for months? Was my cheesecake really that bad?"

James gave her a humourless look as he twiddled with his hearing-aid controls. "Actually, Clarence and Bert seem to be missing. I thought you might have run into them?"

She shook her head slowly.

"I normally would not be worried." He twiddled a hearing aid. "It is just that I lent them money."

———

Before the pandemic, the three old men had been among her best customers. They didn't have much in common other than remaining alive when so many of their contemporaries had dropped off the perch, but they came at least once a day, drank tea, dunked their biscuits and squabbled.

But like a lot of older people, they had stopped visiting the cafe.

As much as she needed the business, she could not blame them.

The Wind Tunnel Cafe was an imposing, colourful building with large windows at the front and one side. But it was a bit like a reverse Tardis. Inside was smaller than it looked from outside, and there had only ever been room for two tables. Social-distancing restrictions limited the cafe to just three customers at a time now and to enter they had to log in by smartphone with a QR code.

———

"Bert caught me in a weak moment," James said. "He visited me at my cottage and told me Clarence did not want me to know he had cancer."

Oodles had cancer? This was news to her, which was another consequence of the pandemic. Wendy used to be first to hear the town gossip, before even the hairdressing salon got wind of it. But fewer customers meant fewer wagging tongues.

"I am worried now they might have done a runner with my money," James said. "I have heard of old people going on cruises so they can die in style, but I thought all the ships were tied up in port at the moment."

"I'm sure Oodles and Wish-Wash will turn up, love." She paused. "Just what kind of cancer does poor Oodles have, anyway?"

He adjusted a hearing aid. "Do I look like a doctor?"

"Well, he looked fine the day you all came out of your quarantine — before he succumbed to food poisoning, anyway."

"Did you have to remind me?"

"So, how much did you lend them?" Her voice dropped back into huskiness.

"We could have died because of that man's actions."

"Dave Jenkins didn't even attend your coming-out party. He was conducting a funeral."

"Yes, well, we will see about that flimsy alibi. If you must know, Bert said Clarence was too proud to tell me he needed help paying his medical bills."

Her voice dropped even more. "How much did you lend him?"

"I am now thinking too much."

"How much?"

"OK, but this is just between us. Ten-thousand dollars."

"Ten-thousand dollars!" Wendy started coughing and spluttering. Everyone knew James had money hidden away in family accounts, even though he claimed to have lost all his dough in a bad investment. But ten thousand dollars? She only dreamed of having that kind of money. The cafe needed repainting and she could really do with a holiday.

Now there was no Gordo, fetching the mail from the Post Office fell to her, and the short trek to next door was the nearest to a holiday she got these days.

The only time she got to relax was when she took the letters back to the cafe and opened them over her first cup of tea and her third cigarette for the day. If they were bills, that might call for a fourth cigarette.

———

James studied the return addresses on both of his letters before unzipping his briefcase and putting them inside. "I need to attend to this mail as soon as possible."

"Should I be worried about this development?" Wendy said.

"I am sure you will find out about it in the fullness of time." He lifted his head. "You will have to excuse me. I am very busy. Amongst other things, I need to go to the police station as soon as it opens this morning. Clarence's and Bert's suspicious disappearance is just another thing I have to raise with Sergeant Stretch."

"But . . .?"

"A merry Christmas to you." He bowed his head, then turned and trotted back around the corner.

———

Wendy resumed the search for the keys in her handbag. She sifted through lipsticks, tissues, hair bands, hair brushes, breath mints, fingernail polish, cigarette packet and matches before she found them.

She bent down, opened P.O. Box 32, on the bottom of three rows, and saw a letter waiting inside.

She took it out and turned it over to see who had sent it.

Kipling and Howard Property Management Pty Ltd.

She sighed and dropped the unopened letter into her bag. Don't say they were raising the rent again!

AUTHOR'S NOTE

THIS NOVEL WAS CALLED *Apples* when I first wrote it in 1993. I say *first* wrote it because I overhauled it big-time to bring it into the digital age.

That happened in 2016 after my career as a journalist came to an abrupt, premature end.

I was 55 and wondered what I could do now.

I found the answer in some boxes of old unsold books in my garage — a link to another crossroad in my career.

In 1993 I had just finished a two-year stint as chief-of-staff on a Tasmanian newspaper. I decided to have a crack at writing a novel to fill in all those extra hours I now had.

The craftwork wasn't particularly good but I had learned the skills to be a disciplined writer able to meet any deadlines I set. I had also come across plenty of interesting character types in my time as a journalist, so my well of ideas was deep.

I also had the skills to manage the production of the book at a local printery.

This is where it came to a grinding halt — a bit like a train that had reached the end of the track!

I had paid for 500 copies to be printed and quickly realised it wasn't time to give up my day job.

The only cheap way to get my books into stores was to load up my car with copies and drive around the state with a hit list, then stop and beg. I lived on an island — so my potential market was quite limited — and I'm terrible at begging.

I sold a few copies and barely covered my costs. Though if we factor in petrol and the wear and tear on my car, I'm probably still in the red.

There is a happy ending to this story.

I was able to treat *Apples* as a first draft for the *Who Knew Tasmanian Tigers Eat Apples!*

This book has now found its way into more than 80 countries.

FINALLY

This novel has been professionally edited. If you've got this far my guess is you've successfully navigated the Australian spelling, slang and deliberate oddities. But typos always manage to slip through the net, so by all means let me know if something's out of order.

– John Martin
https://johnmartin-author.blog

MY BOOKS

Windy Mountain series

Lie of the Tiger (#1)

He's not who he says he is. Who will rescue him?

———

Blokes on a Plane (#2)

Why is the mayor speaking old English? And where has he disappeared to?

_____

Whitey and the Six Dwarfs (#3)

Troupe of Elvis impersonators come to the rescue.

———

Blokes in Donegal (#4)

Three old blokes go to Ireland hoping to discover family history. The mayor had to take his great, great, great grandfather's head, didn't he!

———

Blokes in the House (#5)

How the old blokes coped with COVID quarantine (clue: the major didn't).

———

Who Knew Tasmanian Tigers Eat Apples. (#6)

Back to before the beginning. Wish-Wash leads a public revolt.

———

Who Knew Tiger Sharks also Eat Apples? (#7)

A character from the old days returns in an unlikely guise. It's all about comic revenge.

———

The Life and Deaths of Billy Gumboots (#8)

'His foot, my boot.'

_____

Blokes Send in the Clones (#9)

Two old blokes have a crack at cloning a Tasmanian tiger.

To come:

10 — Blokes do the Block

Someone marries, someone dies. Might even be the same old bloke.

———

Funny Capers DownUnder series

The Wrong Magician (#1)

This time he has to make himself disappear.

———

Daddy's Great Escape (#2)

If Mad Bill hates people so much, why does he make it so hard for them to leave his island?

———

Escape from Mad Bill's Island (#3)

He came seeking to find out what the British were up to on the island in World War 2. He won't like the answer.

———

Standalone novels

Major B.S. comes to the end of his Rope

It all started when he rescued the wrong group of people from a prisoner-of-war camp. It just becomes worse.

———